Human Being Songs

Human Being Songs

Northern Stories

Jean Anderson

UNIVERSITY OF ALASKA PRESS

Published by
University of Alaska Press
P.O. Box 756240
Fairbanks, AK 99775-6240

Cover design: Jen Gunderson, 590 Design
Cover image: *Tussock Trekkers*. Cast bronze sculpture by Wendy Ernst Croskrey. Photo by Wendy Ernst Croskrey
Interior design: Rachel Fudge

Stories in this book previously appeared—some in slightly different form—in the following publications: "Profligate" in *Connotations*, "Counting" in *Kalliope*, "Snobs" in *The Alaska Reader: Voices from the North* (Fulcrum Publishing) as well as *Prairie Schooner* and *Papergraders: Notes from the Academic Underclass* (Cairn Press), "Thaw" in *Chariton Review*, "The Immediate Jewel" in *Connotations*, "Blizzard" in *Northern Review*, "Smallpox" in *Ginosko* and *Sugar Mule*, "Air" in *Northern Review*, "Cats and Dogs" in *Alaska Women Speak*, and "Contagion" in *Chariton Review*.

Thanks to Cornell University Press for use of a line from A.R. Ammons' poem "Terrain" (*Selected Poems*). Legend in the story "Thaw" from *Unangam Ungiikangin Kayax Tunusangin: Aleut Tales and Narratives* (collected 1909–1910 by Waldemar Jochelson, edited by Knut Bergsland and Moses Dirks, Fairbanks: Alaska Native Language Center, 1990). Details from the life of Ioann Veniaminov in the story "Blizzard" from *A Good and Faithful Servant* (University of Alaska Press, 1997). Song lyric in the opening lines of the story "Human Being Songs" from the traditional ballad "The Unquiet Grave."

Library of Congress Cataloging in Publication Data

Names: Anderson, Jean, 1940 author.
Title: Human being songs : northern stories / Jean Anderson.
Description: Fairbanks, Alaska : University of Alaska Press, 2017. | Includes bibliographical references.
Identifiers: LCCN 2016025379 (print) | LCCN 2016034124 (ebook) | ISBN 9781602233133 (pbk. : alk. paper) | ISBN 9781602233140 ()
Classification: LCC PS3551.N368 A6 2017 (print) | LCC PS3551.N368 (ebook) | DDC 813/.54dc23
LC record available at https://lccn.loc.gov/2016025379

This collection is dedicated to those who know they have a book in them,
or a second one or a third, and to our Mighty Seven:
Michael, Nicholas, Sam, David, John, Ava, Elysa.

Contents

Acknowledgments

This small book was many years in the making, and I'm honored to offer thanks to numerous individuals and groups who helped along the way: to Don, Tom, Laura, and all my family for decades of support; to Peggy Shumaker for her generosity and vision, and to James Engelhardt and Amy Simpson and the staff at the University of Alaska Press for kindness and encouragement; to Marge Piercy for selecting this collection as a finalist for the 2015 G.S. Sharat Chandra Prize for Short Fiction from BkMk Press at the University of Missouri-Kansas City and for her personal kindness; to Wendy Croskrey, whose postcard image of her sculpture *Tussock Trekkers* inspired me through the writing of so many of these stories; to students and staff in the Lower Kuskokwim School District for hospitality and inspiration during a long-ago visit; and to editors and staff members at the journals and anthologies who selected and published these stories.

Many friends shared dreams and offered vision, friendship, and helpful critiques: Marjorie Kowalski Cole, Elyse Guttenberg, Joanne Townsend, Ann Chandonnet, Susan Johnson, Ellen Moore, Claire Fejes, Elizabeth Wales, Yvonne Mozee, Norma and Jerry Bowkett, Leah Aronow-Brown, Birch Pavelsky, Eric Heyne, Carolyn Kremers, Sheila Nickerson, Pat Lambert, Barbara Behan-Smith, Joy DeStefano Haines, Shana Karella, Linden Ontjes, Carolyn Peck, Erin Wahl, David Marusek, Carole Glickfeld, Nancy Lord, Martha Amore, John Mitchell, Stanley Elkin, and Carolyn Servid and Dorik

Mechau at The Island Institute in Sitka, where a monthlong residency in November 1996 meant the world to me. Dog Scout was a beloved companion through many years. Last but among my most heartfelt thank-yous go to my friends in the Writers League, who read and strengthened so many of these stories: Susan Campbell, Burns Cooper, Cindy Hardy, Susheila Khera, John Kooistra, John Morgan, and Linda Schandelmeier. Go little book.

Love's mysteries in souls do grow,
But yet the body is his book.

—John Donne, "The Ecstasy"

Profligate

My mother carries her money in a plastic baggie. Sitting next to me on the blue plush plane seat, she extracts a shiny transparent lump from her purse and unzips it to count currency into the steward's girlish hand: separate coins like raisins or buttons in the cool darkness of the plane, U.S. dollar bills neatly folded as Kleenex.

She's buying us each a Maui Mai Tai, her idea but the young steward's suggestion. Odd, since her strongest lifelong alcoholic beverage of choice has been beer, tiny amounts sipped warm from a teacup, when I was a child at least, for her pleurisy. She first asked the steward for two Bloody Marys but then decided she doesn't care that much for Spicy Tom—do I?

I'm shaking my head, and the steward, who is barely twenty-one if my guess is accurate, appears to be flirting with my mother. Who is seventy-four years plus ten days—this trip is a birthday gift. The drinks and the flirting seem a blend, elaborate hand and body motions like a dance in place in the dark aisle from the steward, then a bottled juice called Fruitopia, over ice, poured with rum from two tiny bottles into two plastic cups, and pineapple chunks speared on long, elegant toothpicks. I'm thinking all at once, and I don't know why, of how much Siberians love Ziploc bags, how they save them, use them for everything, but not plastic cups. The steward leaves us the tiny bottles of rum, twirls his fingers at my mother before he begins to push his heavy cart down the aisle, commanding us airily: "Enjoy!" And I know suddenly, though who knows why, or why this, or why now, that I too never have been—no, and probably never will be—profligate. Mom worried over that tendency in me once, I think: that her toothy daughter who drank milk like water during and after meals all through childhood would turn out to be profligate.

We're flying to Hawaii from Anchorage—cheap off-season tickets that include three days in a close-to-the-beach hotel, my treat but my mother's lifelong dream. It's the first trip to Hawaii for each of us, Mom's second time on an airplane, and I'm not yet thinking of Aeroflot, which I always do these days when I fly.

Her first jet flight was a week ago, Cincinnati to Anchorage, where I've lived for a year, to visit me—my twenty-fifth year in Alaska and her first time in the North. My most recent flights were to Cincinnati then back to Anchorage with Mom, one week ago, then on to Fairbanks together by car to visit my sons, and to treeless and windy Bethel in southwest Alaska three weeks earlier, alone, to teach dental hygiene techniques to nurses at the regional hospital. Before that, the chopped-up remains of Aeroflot: the Russian Far East, and then Siberia, which I love—six weeks teaching the same courses over and over, in Magadan, rainy Khabarovsk, Petropavlovsk, then Sakha, in or around Yakutsk.

These are words, places, even skills I never expected to find in my life, and all have come in the last three years: divorce, Anchorage, Siberia, dental hygiene education, and *zoobastay* ("large-toothed" in Russian)—a long-term health advantage I'd always viewed in my own case, in my own mouth, as a disadvantage—so ugly-looking—and now death. Again. Maybe Mom and I will learn to be profligate, facing death.

"Do you miss Dad?" I ask that while we sip at our Maui Mai Tais, and she stops sipping to answer. She places her plastic cup on my fold-down tray, which we're sharing, touches her chin with a fingertip and her thumb—newly gnarled and yet beautiful, fingers still beautiful, a hand so loved, so amazingly familiar to my eyes that I feel shocked by the sight: nearly as well-known as my own fingers and hand.

"*Miss* is an odd word, isn't it?" she answers.

"I miss him sometimes," I say. "Funny I guess, since we were together so seldom, Russell and I living in Alaska." Because they never visited me. Not once over the years. Travel a reckless behavior that Dad seemed to consider impossible. "But I do miss him."

"His jokes," she says.

"That's it for me too." What Dad would have said, always a joke, about this or that.

"He wouldn't have liked this," she says, lifting her plastic cup and sipping. "Do they really drink so much as the newspapers say? In Russia?"

"Not the people I've met. Statistically though." I'm nodding. "It's a big problem. For Alaskans too. Maybe the climate."

"Drinking's one way you can break free, I suppose. But then people drink in Hawaii too, don't they? I read that in a travel book." She's smiling again, sipping. "This is very sweet. Too sweet for you?"

I'm shaking my head. I can hardly believe what Mom's doctor told my sister Lorraine last month: metastasized, profligate cells, no treatment possible, less than a year. And that he thinks Mom already knows. He feels certain she knows, after all her surgeries. That there's no need to tell her, he thinks. She wouldn't want to be told in words. It would be too difficult, too painful for all.

She looks pretty good to me, almost well. Dark and mysterious-looking as always: "pretty," yet elusive. Bittersweet, a secretive look, and not gray at all. But pale and thin. But then she's always been thin. And white-skinned. Dark and yet fair—as I am. And as inconsistent. Timid-seeming then startlingly bold, each of us. But she wanted to come—to see Alaska, then fly on to Hawaii. I'm thinking that: she wanted to.

"He was proud of you." She's speaking of Dad again I know, her mind filled with shifts and curves like my own. "Did you know that?"

I'm hunting for words, but she's going on. "He wasn't so—*easy* a man as most people thought. But he never did mind not having sons."

Then: "Those neighbor girls—Brianna and Mallory? They remind me of you and Sis. They'd like the taste of this." She lifts the plastic glass like a toast to the dark air of the cabin and sips. She's wearing her new wedding band, the one Dad gave her for their fiftieth anniversary three years ago. Her first wedding band, with its faint tracery of orange blossoms on the delicate braiding of the band, which I loved to look at as a child, had worn through and split with age.

Rather than sell the house our sons grew up in, Russell and I rented it to the oldest, to Mitchell and his family, after we divorced. Two years ago. Mom and I stayed there for our three days in Fairbanks last week, like campers in my former home, with Mitch and Abby and their baby girls— my grandchildren, Melissa and Daisy, an infant and a toddler. That week brought Mom her first real sight of her great-granddaughters. Mom and I slept in the little-girl bedroom, Daisy's now, that was Mitch's room once, then the guest room.

It was eerie for me sleeping there, pasts and futures shuffled together like a game of cards in the midnight sun, the way things often feel in Siberia during their White Nights, or even in winter. Change in the air there: Alaska-in-Asia, the Russian Far East—home but not home at all. Which may be one reason I love it. But eerie, like Mom's first visit to my former home, the house I lived in and loved for twenty years, then suddenly hated.

And Mallory is my former neighbor, a tomboy and nonstop talker who's eight years old and always rides up breathless on her pint-sized boy's bike, with her six-year-old cousin Brianna pedaling hard behind on her own pink bike. They're part of a big Athabascan family, my neighbors for years till Russell and I divorced. Through two marriages for Mallory's mother and with more births and deaths in their clan than I could count or even remember if I tried.

The girls came to visit Mom, to talk, every day during our few days in Fairbanks, just as Mallory and her older sister Lauren used to visit me when I lived there. They'd show up like clockwork on their tiny bikes back then, often at mealtime—Russell hated it—sometimes twice a day or more often. So Mom already knew them in a way, Mallory's family, from my phone calls and letters over the years.

"Did they show you how they make raspberry jam?" Mom is smiling and I'm shaking my head again.

"Mallory and Brianna?" Mom saw them, I didn't, like the dancers from Yakutsk, the Sakha Circus at the Tanana Valley Fair in Fairbanks last week—even sandhill cranes that nest in summer in Siberia flying overhead while they danced. I've probably missed Mallory, and the wild cranes and the birch woods and that raspberry patch at the end of our driveway, as much as any-thing else since I left.

How strange the human heart is, I'm thinking: selecting, rejecting. And I'm wondering if all females—all humans, maybe—are as wanton in their loyalties as Mom and I always have been. Hearts profligate, then suddenly closed as a fist.

"In a plastic baggie," Mom says, placing her cup on my tray again. She's illustrating the process—milking a cow—with hands I'm already missing; a pang in my heart, watching her hands. "They're careful about the berries. Only the best ones, Mallory says. They put them in a baggie and seal it, squeeze the bag, then pour off the juice by unsealing it at one side. Seems like they'd save the juice." She stops to sip. "Wasteful not to. But Mallory says you can't use everything, it's impossible, and Brianna says it's too messy to drink, the jam is the best part anyway. It's the Indian way, Mallory says."

"Why didn't you come before?" I ask. "Even if Dad wouldn't, you could've come."

Her father's family was full of riverboat captains. Her maternal grandparents crossed the ocean from Ireland and Germany as teenagers—each alone—exhilarated, terrified, who knows? They met on board the ship and later married, worked for years together as domestics in Boston, then traveled to Cincinnati in a covered wagon, where Mom's grandfather became a Methodist preacher—then her father, his youngest son-in-law and no riverman. When the first radios appeared—voices and wild talk pouring out of that box on the kitchen table when Mom was a child—her father, a careful man, climbed onto the roof of the shed to find the pranksters (his own children?) throwing their voices like that. He died in his forties, suddenly, a year or two later, never sick, leaving Grandma a widow with four skinny children and then three. Mom and her older sister and brother rarely left Cincinnati.

Homebodies, as people used to say. Like Dad's generation, whose grandparents all made their way slowly from Germany. In groups or else one by one—carefully maybe, or boldly? Making music on shipboard, I suspect. Conversationalists, friendly and weighty and gentle. Witty like Dad, who was so—*sociable*, fond of people and music and beer. Fond of home. Such a stubbornly rooted and stubbornly loving man—despite or because of losing his father at ten? Despite or because of that terrifying and tragic departure? His father collapsing at home, in the yard, after a full day's work. Death lurked like an Eastern Orthodox icon in our family when I was a child, perched high in a shadowy corner waiting to strike again. But maybe nobody ever saw it but me?

Those first U.S. generations on Dad's side were full of musicians and craftsmen, cabinetmakers, free of the factories that later claimed Dad and his brothers. Can you stay alive, as I'd like to believe, in your work? In human teeth? Or in those family treasures Dad's father made? Mom's kept them: two beautiful polished chairs and that small chest—wood like silk—for Sis and me now. In Cincinnati, home by then. Speaking English only: *Americans*, never again to be forced to roam—except maybe by war.

I've roamed—gone West, as so many others did all those generations ago, to new worlds we never imagined. Geography, beyond the new millennium's bend, has coaxed me so far West I've gone East. Maybe like digging a hole in the backyard and reaching China. Not really intending it, never exactly "brave."

But I've loved it. My best self is a traveler, I've learned that. And which part of me *is* myself now? Which part USA, Cincinnati, Alaska, Fairbanks, Anchorage, and now Siberia and the Russian Far East?

And how can it be that my mother will never see the winters I've learned with such difficulty to endure, then to love? And how can time move so cruelly, leaping the heart's tallest fences again and again, anyplace, everywhere?

But maybe places and climates, nations, geographies, time—even death—aren't factors in a heart's equation at all? Maybe loving, finding ways to be happy, ways to *be*—making music and prayers and beautiful objects, making children, making a life—maybe these are always a heart's only defense? The bravest and most profligate human actions of all, anytime, anywhere? Maybe that's the wisdom my mother is offering me with her tale of berries?

"I'm here now, Kitty," Mom says. "We'll learn the hula together, won't we? Won't that be fun?" She's smiling again. Nobody has called me Kitty for years. And, sipping at her Maui Mai Tai, my mother pats my hand while we enter the higher sky.

Counting: A Tale of Enumeration

. . . the soul is a region without definite boundaries . . .
—A.R. Ammons, "Terrain"

Did it all begin with Pal Hennessey's dog? With Jasmine? *PERSON 1: JASMINE?*

Had she (Maurie to friends) already started to slip (by then, on her second or third day?) away from the absolute, the numerical, the wholly and entirely factual? Toward the holy, the hole-filled, the whole—beginning with that fat, elderly matted ball of fluff?

JASMINE (the name on its tag): a dog wearing a pink bandanna kerchief, its collar hooked to a rusty chain it pulls down and up the muddy plank steps of the trailer, switching its tail, bouncing its head, its entire off-white self ashimmy, back end gyrating, thudding—front/hind/middle waggling in paroxysms of joy to announce it without any words and only two or three ear-splitting yips: *Somebody's come to visit at last!*

Or with Pal himself, 83, Jasmine named by his dear departed Madge. Married sixty-two years, both listed on their card, one around here someplace. Yes, slightly bent—tucked under a corner of the full-up sofa: "You'll enjoy it, missie."

Pal offered the card grandly, and she *did* accept, has kept it, treasures in fact that only slightly soiled emblem of triumph made up when they retired in Michigan, he and Madge.

Their out-of-business card before they came up to Alaska:

HENNESSEYS UNLEASHED

Did it start with that feeling of home and Pal standing bent forward, hunched over to open the door? Body English to his welcome it seems, calling her in with a grand sweep of his fine big hands: both hands. Into a dark nest of stacked magazines everywhere, boxes labeled and un-, beside or atop the quilts, crocheted throws, so many objects folded or spread or tossed. And hand tools, bits of metal or wood, coffee cups, empty saucer-size plates, newspapers, rounds of electric cord or black electrical tape, stubs of pencils and so many ballpoint pens. Small mounds of stuff tossed down beside scrawled-looking notes (to himself?) and torn envelopes bearing more scrawls.

"Stuff, stuff, stuff everyplace," exactly as Pal (her own tall height, still hunched) phrases it: "Don't mind the mess, missie. Come in, come in."

So that the only empty space is the one she must fill: his quilt-covered La-Z-Boy.

"No, no," Maureen *does* say (if memory serves), "I don't want to take your—" while she shuffles her clipboard and maps and the handful of census forms.

But he insists, of course: "Have a seat. Best chair in the house, missie." Ignoring her protests, sweeping those fine big hands again, appreciating she knows the sight of her eyes going soft (pupils dilating in the half-dark) and her smiles, smiles, smiles-in-spite-of-herself to meet a kindred.

Ah, yes, who wouldn't start with Pal? A man leaning into his own booming voice, lovely music, talk-as-dance to Pal: "Be at home, please, missie, and do excuse the house. Such a sight even the dog won't come in anymore. And I have no excuse. Mother taught me. I was youngest of ten and her right hand at housework, so I do know how. And a taskmaster she was, Mother! No sloughing off for Mother. She'd shame me for the state of this place."

So that they both already know more truths—each about each, maybe (for she does feel that Pal knows her too, but how?)—than any census form could ever hold or even request.

Did it start with that question: How do you know essentials at once? Personality, dreams, a bit of IQ, lover or not, power mad or not—how do you know? Pal's tenderness, his weakness for the ladies, his kindness, how lonesome he is. And her own prissiness layered atop some far more basic, equally hopeless longing or lust or hunger for so many irresistible morsels of life's everyday feast that she (too) must often pluck them out of thin air.

Yet it *is* the first thing you always do know, of course, or think you do (however it's known), that essence. Then, as you dance into it with a bit of talk, sometimes you see you were wrong. Or else maybe a bit off, but not totally wrong. Somehow you *do* know right away. So many things beyond the bare facts. Things no one could ever fit onto the forms.

And yes, anyway, you must start someplace, and here with Pal was surely one of the finest: she knew it then as well as she knows it now. Besides, nobody's called her missie for ten years at least, maybe twenty. And Pal was or is—but what? What exactly?

A big man, very tall, overweight, deep-voiced, witty, very kind. Friendly, full of life, full of fun, and handsome still, despite his years and the indignities imposed by his spine: a visible gnarling and crumbling of bones, which anybody can see has forced his elegant crouch. From which he lifts himself nobly again to joke. To talk, wave an arm, a hand, to smile and smile while he gestures again and again, face or body or hands, standing through the whole short form interview. (Bent over in pain?) Ignoring her soon-to-be-usual deadly introduction: she has back trouble (too) and doesn't mind standing, and so on, and the short form takes only ten minutes at most—

"Too bad," answers Pal. "Not the long one? We just get the short one?"

While she sits anyway (aching) as he insists, goes on a bit about spring, says what a nice court this is, so homey, people so friendly—and the trees! Breaking census rules, chatting away as always, being personal, sitting in his sprung but still fairly comfy chair.

Yes, it must have begun with Pal: "Reginald Dylan really—isn't it awful?" (For his mother's brother who died an infant.) "How *could* Mother do that to me? Though with nine others to name I guess she'd used up all the good ones by then."

∾

Or, if you'd prefer, let it start with Jasmine. Since, as Pal joked (which they all did, or nearly all the decent ones anyway, as Maureen will find out very soon): "That dog should be counted too since she runs the place."

∾

Or, since you must start someplace, let it start with herself as the forms require it: *PERSON 1: BOSWELL, MAUREEN C.* in legible caps. After the *RECORD OF CONTACT, CERTIFICATION, INTRODUCTION* on the enumerator form.

Let it start exactly as the dark-print instructions phrase it. ("Exact words, and you'd best use 'em," said her trainers, Arlen at first and then Betts, nodding in unison. "Think of it as U.S. Census syntax," said Arlen. "First rev up your ol' bod' for the job, then plunge in with exact census-form words. And use 'em. Every one, one by one. Memorize each and every exact word, or you jest might wade off into deep doo-doo. . . .")

("Or start things off on the wrong foot, let's say," said Betts. "And no chit-chat.") *WHAT IS EACH PERSON'S NAME? START WITH THE NAME OF A PERSON WHO OWNS, IS BUYING, OR RENTS THIS (HOUSE/APARTMENT/MOBILE HOME).*

"But why, in the twenty-first century, do census rules require us to start from a site rather than a person? Why not a person?" Maureen asked that. If this is a real census, a head count, an enumeration of citizen-souls to step boldly forth into the complex future, *why?* That was her thought.

"Because you have to start someplace," Betts said.

And Arlen agreed: "Who are we," asked Arlen, "to quarrel with the feds? Ours not to reason why. Twenty-five bucks an hour, keep on thinking that."

∾

Or did it begin with Bert Kirbe? Unknown neighbor to Pal—single too, and nearer her own age. Home at last on her fourth or fifth try.

A bit overweight, but not bad, tall—with that gorgeous long-legged, silky-haired tricolor cat. Who accompanies Maureen from the car, has accompanied her forward and back each time, every visit (she's already left two notification of contact forms), across the loveliest yard she's seen.

His two-story cabin-house like an aging Swiss chalet set down in the not-quite forest, hidden in thin woods below the trailer court. Birch trees in full leaf and the spring runoff creek in the yard nearly dry, a warped board angled across it. Over a stone path that leads to a sunny deck with an umbrella table and two white-painted wrought-iron chairs settled among objects she could live with: history of Alaska, tidbits of Europe, and so many actual books! (Through the windows she's seen them: that wall of bookcases filled with a lovely wealth of books.) Each visit her small vacation to this kingdom so perfectly home but never imagined before.

Bert in the kitchen, a Saturday midday, robins singing, sunny, warm, springtime in Fairbanks, and he's scrubbing at bright yellow counter tiles with a toothbrush. The side door's wide open, bleach smells fill the porch, and his nice voice sends forth words even before he can see her: "God! This stuff's knocking me for a loop," says Bert.

As a greeting? ("Ah—hello." Was that Maureen's clever answer?)

Robert, though he's called Bert. "No, no, not the long form!" He objects, lifting both arms tragically and the toothbrush. (Another refusal? Damn! After so many tries! But—would she answer herself? When her own short form came in the mail last month, before she decided to take the test and apply for this job, she herself nearly balked.)

"Too damned nosy," says Bert. "What right do they have?"

She can't say her speech again, stays silent beside the cat, gets ready to leave. Then she thinks of a final ploy. A fact: "Well, I do think they can actually fine you." That gets his attention. His graying eyebrows lift. "Two hundred dollars, I think."

Then, from Bert: "How little of it can we do? What's the least they'll accept?" Quick answers to the first few pages, co-conspirators, while she stands in the doorway bent over her clipboard and he sways busily, in and out of the bleach fumes, wielding toothbrush on ceramic tiles.

Disinterested or just self-contained? Or is doing this much his way to show faint (personal?) interest? Nothing here *personal*, of course. Only the questions: that's always their stated objection (as from Bert) when they object. Besides, it's the house she likes, all those books. And his cat.

But. Is he divorced? A widower? Gay?

And why can she always imagine another life? Or ten others at once, elbowing out the real? (For she *does* have a real.) Like a sixteen-year-old, still. Let me count the ways.

Cat strolls with her again as she leaves, back-rubbing Maureen's ankles across a trickle of streambed. At the car, another friendly *meow* as good-bye from cat.

~

Just down the road a bit, the Arkansas hills. Dogs sit on box houses, small and big, chickens cluck through mud and the start of a garden.

Though Grace and Joseph have never lived there. Not Arkansas yet, no. They've lived plenty of other places, in Alaska only two years. They'll do the long form.

"But no questions we consider too—" says he. Maureen understands.

World War II as an underage teen for Joseph: he lied about his age. He's disabled, Grace too, a bit. She's white-haired, soft-skinned, healthy looking, very lively, slim. Only 54! A shock for Maureen: younger than herself!

No plumbing, two rooms, wood heat, cabin rented: "Our own screen door." (Grace's joke, but they both chuckle.) To keep in needle-tooth pup Grace holds on her lap, and the cats: "And, we hope, to keep out some 'skee-toes," says Grace. Joseph's a very youthful 81, Grace part American Indian, Cherokee: Joseph so proud to tell it Grace blushes.

Joseph is Dutch, German, English, French—several others too, he thinks.

Some high school for him, fifth grade for her. No kids. ("'Cept her." Joseph's joke, but it's Grace who laughs.) Married thirty-two years.

And they're lovers.

Maureen knows it suddenly—almost blushing when it leaps to mind as she pencils her marks onto the forms. Forms gliding like dancers on oilcloth on their kitchen table, country music on the radio, jokes, one cigarette they share. Joseph with his bad limp, nearly blind, no work since 1994, and Grace:

too playful, too shy, too sexy still, too ready with that quick chime of slightly too-loud girlish laughter to not be loved.

She's never worked, Grace says. They get disability (exact amount refused) and Maureen thinks this: *I still do know happiness when I see it.*

The rest of their form is her prayer for them: *Let it last.*

⁓

All the rest is embroidery: Bill Whacht, 48 though he looks 35, cooking Polish sausages for supper in the cabin he's been building for years, ten or twelve so far. Cooking indoors in the rain on an outdoor grill.

"Cabin's so badly caulked it's no problem," he says. "Fumes no problem at all." Two stories, two rooms, four picture windows lining the bare walls in the unfinished bottom one where they stand. The view out over the valley towards Fox: *Ah, yes, Heaven.*

And Wallace Till with his waxed mustache, his offer of a beer and their pleasant chat doing the long form outside his tiny house while the sun shines like midafternoon at nine thirty p.m. as his friendly tenants come and go to their tiny house beside his. The two structures are unattached, separate houses, he says, though they look to Maureen like Siamese twins.

Two unlinked and unplumbed homes at the top of the hill over-looping Heaven near Bill Whacht's half-built home. Robins and lilacs, spruce trees and willows, birch too in the yard, while mosquitoes attack in clouds and Wallace, 41, never married, tells Maureen she's a very nice lady. ("'Scuse me, I've had several beers.") As his geriatric cat and elderly dog both beg to be petted: "Ignore 'em," says Wallace. "Our turn now."

Then young-looking widow Marie Stetzer, 49, just back from her husband's funeral.

Congressional Medal of Honor, Washington, DC. Neighbors saw her on TV. Yes, killed in action. "Last year, very hard. Just hasn't sunk in yet—anything. Not quite real." Only herself living here now, kids grown up. Though her son checks on her, leaves urine in those plastic bottles on the path (did Maureen see them?) for the bears. She apologizes for forgetting to send in her form.

And Ilze Tremont, 54, in her big suburban house, trying to call long distance to her mother's nursing home in Michigan. About to fly off for the emergency, trying not to cry while she gives quick answers in response to the short form. Calling out to offer aspirins ("for your back") as Maureen limps away down the driveway.

And Jo Minot, 51, so pretty, eating the last of last year's salmon from the freezer with wild blueberry jam on biscuits, licking her fingertips daintily while she thanks Maureen "for doing our census. It's very important work and it must be a challenge at times."

"Oh, thank you," answers Maureen. "How kind of you to say that! But most people are nice. I haven't been shot at yet." (Though her co-workers call the big red *CENSUS* buttons they must wear pinned to their chests "our targets.")

And the very shy Iñupiaq wife, Matilda Jones, 44, packing, getting ready to drive south in the family's station wagon, leaving their small log house for the summer. With her schoolteacher husband and their five young children—to visit his family in Indiana.

And the Bush teacher who comes each summer from Newtok (he was enumerated already, at school)—permafrost thawing there, homes swallowed up by global warming—to live at the sunny, big-treed end of a rutted muddy road: Whistling Swan Drive. In a wishbone-shaped metal cabin: a curved-legged inverted V pulled out maybe twenty feet like an accordion, walls and ceiling sprayed with urethane painted deepest robin's-egg blue: "God's favorite color, according to Russian Orthodox Yup'iks," he tells Maureen.

And Maureen's son's childhood friend Danny, 37, a stay-at-home dad and glad to see her in the half-finished house he's building despite his ruined back. "Awful today. Too many years as a mechanic. Worse since the surgery, even the pills can't touch it most days." Joking that he and his children are still "half-a-basket. No, no, not Athabascan."

And the sexy, young, very short-haired, very dark-skinned man with a red-haired, very white-skinned baby astride his hip, moving boxes into Pal's trailer court, two streets below Pal. At home on her second or third try, and the first Negro she's seen in this court. (Does Maureen only imagine neighbors peeking out windows? Neighbors *did* scowl when she asked if anyone lived here. Racists? In Pal's so-friendly-seeming trailer court?)

No, he didn't live here on April first, and he sent in his form at the other place. He thinks this trailer's been empty all winter. She might try the guy who rents out trailers.

Maureen talks then to the manager's wife, in a very nice trailer down the way: her dad just finished with triple bypass, yes, successful, in Seattle. She's been out of town for the surgery, hasn't kept up with rentals for weeks, sorry. Try Hank, her husband, home late evenings only: he's working every possible daylight hour on their new house.

Hank's friendly, brisk, in charge, with both a thick gold-nugget ring and a thicker watchband he's proud to flash. There's a *PALIN IN '12* bumper sticker on his truck, and: "Yes, it's been empty for three or four months, that trailer, C-8. Nobody there in April."

And the two proudly Hispanic families, two husbands, two fathers (*PERSON 1*: 24, son-in-law to *PERSON 3*: 51), two wives and mothers (53, wife to *PERSON 3*, mother to *PERSON 2*—who's 22 and daughter to *PERSONS 3 AND 4*, wife to *PERSON 1*: parents of two children, 3 years and 2 months, *PERSONS 5 AND 6*) all (happily? so it seems to Maureen) stuffed into one single-wide trailer a block or so from Pal, and joking: "*PERSON 1*—or would that be *PERSON 3*?" The young man who answered the door is looking over Maureen's shoulder: "Maybe it should be *4*?"

"But Daddy, there's five of us," chirps the bright-eyed little boy who's appeared.

Daddy's insisting meanwhile that, yes, *PERSON 1, OWNER*, should be his wife's father. "Right here, *PERSON 1*," not himself: "Good thing it's in pencil. Yes, right here." (*PERSON 1* is a tattoo-covered bandy-legged guy with a gray ponytail who's just come to the door: scary-looking to Maureen.)

"No, six now, Billy," says Grandpa (*PERSON 1*), bouncing a beautiful baby against his chest: "You forgot sister."

And Carlton Willis, 56, hauling groceries into a trailer across the street. Somber-eyed son, Shawn, 7, who listens carefully as his father can't help but sing out his woes: "What a month! Let me look back at the calendar." Wife, much younger, 31, she's not living here now. No, not on the first of April, only himself and Shawn then: "Alone together on census day: April Fools," shaking his head. Himself and son. "Had to put her out, actually. That's it, no choice. An awful thing" (from this spotless trailer? but who keeps—or kept it? Maureen wonders that in silence) while he apologizes for the state of the place, shaking his head again, calling it a wreck: "Everything's in such turmoil." (But it's very clean.)

"Bars, maybe drugs," he says, "running around with men. Went on for months. Just about killed me to put her out. Didn't care at the last whether I knew or not. Even brought men back here a few times. Too young for me, maybe. But I loved her. I sure as heck tried."

He'll sell the trailer if he can (there's a *FOR SALE* sign in the window) to pay the lawyer, try to win custody: "Just can't see Shawn raised like that." He shakes his head again sadly: "God, wish me luck."

Maureen's familiar with divorce—she's a widow herself, but a long-time, part-time legal secretary, doing the census (as she likes to joke) to escape from the law. So she knows he'll probably lose custody of the child. Maybe lose everything, even this spotless trailer. But—wish him luck she does.

Then comes Ms. Nameless in her huge, half-million-dollar place—*The Manor House*, Maureen's thinking, as she checks her census map and drives to the top of the hill. But the woman is "far too busy" to do the form. Anyway, she's "utterly sick of them. I've done so many already," the woman says, frowning. "I'm quite familiar with the process. What a nuisance!"

Maureen's petting the friendly black lab on the doorstep, enjoying the gorgeous view (so like the view from her unwashed windows at home)— and this woman is someone more like herself than usual. Feeling generous, maybe magnanimous, Maureen offers to come back tomorrow: Sunday evening? Would that be better? Or an evening next week? (It's the long form, thirty minutes. Twenty if Maureen races through, and close to home.)

"Come Monday. To my office," the woman says. "At my school. I'm principal. I can spare only ten minutes, however. One thirty. It'll have to be quick!"

~

Ms. Nameless will refuse her name (*QUESTION 1*) when Maureen skips lunch for their "appointment." But first she ushers Maureen into "my conference room," then lectures for two or three minutes of the ten she herself allotted, announcing again how many forms she's already done—for "my" school: "What a chore! How sick I am of the census!" Then, imperious, gesturing with a flap of her hand for Maureen to begin, she refuses to give her name.

"My time is valuable too!" says Maureen, hopping up—able to hop again: her back's healed (and her soul too, it sometimes seems) as she's hiked her route. But she's hopping mad now. Furious suddenly. Every hair on her head feels angry, a fury that takes her completely by surprise. Behaving rudely too, probably: she hopes to be rude—scooping up the clipboard and stacks of forms and her census bag, turning away. Yet she hopes her face hasn't turned God's favorite color—or Satan's—as she strides out of "my" conference room. "The Census Bureau will send somebody else to enumerate you!" Maureen calls this over a shoulder as she leaves, then adds, caustic as possible: "Thanks so much for your valuable time!"

More furious than she's been in years, Maureen strides across the school parking lot with her flesh afire: What a joke! What a person! Ms. Nameless, with her name engraved on a brass plate tacked up on her ugly posh house! On the office door too, and plastered all over inside "my" public school! It certainly takes all kinds!

Only later, driving back across town—still throbbing with a fury that's barely begun to cool to white-hot, still trying to quiet her racing heart—will Maureen begin to ask herself question after question: What in the world? What was *that* all about? How did it ever happen? How did it begin? And *why*? Why has this woman shaken her so? Made her so murderously angry? Who is she—*MAUREEN BOSWELL, PERSON 1*—after all? And how has she become such a mystery to herself?

Snobs

Darrin is sitting off to the side, on the floor. Not under the skylight in the public library's waiting area. Not on one of the shiny wooden benches scattered among the delicate indoor trees, but here in the shadows next to a rack filled with brochures. He's waiting to be picked up after school where she told him to wait, yes, but here he can see his mother before she sees him. Here he can think, which he needs to do, maybe figure things out.

Then there he is, the huge kid from math class, coming in at the entrance nearest to Darrin. Darrin's heart races: *the huge, limping kid who mutters,* "*Freak.*" The kid who snarls at him, who pushed him into the lunch table today while Darrin managed, just barely, to quick-step backwards, hard, onto the kid's good foot then turn it all into a joke: "When'll they clear up this ice?" While the huge kid limped on, lumbering away, sneering back over his shoulder to mutter it softly again like he always does: "*Freak.*"

Darrin tries to sink into the cold floor, dips his head, breathing hard, actually panting maybe, but the kid doesn't see him. The kid waves a huge fist at somebody else, limps toward the checkout desk, then turns at the stacks and disappears, and Darrin sighs aloud.

Then there *she* is suddenly: his mother, at the far entrance, too soon. Though she's late as always of course, ten minutes late, wearing her new used parka and looking breathless—red-cheeked, harried, her face somber and serious as usual while she struggles through the big glass doors with the stack of books and the records she's returning.

He guesses his mother must be the only woman left in the world who still checks out—listens to, actually *plays*—the library's ancient phonograph records. Poets reading their own poems, black disks she spins in her classes and also listens to herself, frozen in place sometimes while she washes the dishes at night, listening before she begins grading papers. On the few nights she's not teaching, that is. *And the kid thinks I'm a freak!*

"It's 1992, Mom. Other teachers buy tapes, or CDs." He told her that about a month ago. Because he saw the tapes in a catalog she got in the mail: *Poets Speak.* But she said no, of course. Tapes would be too expensive, that was the reason. He knew it even though she didn't say it: *ochen dorogova*— very expensive, in Russian. She's trying to learn that from the big old shiny-black vinyl records too: Russian. "For Siberian students, dear," an interest she's added since he lived with her last, two years ago.

"The library's recordings are perfectly good, Darrin," she said last month, turning the paper catalog around and around in her hands. She was trying hard not to frown, he could tell. "Wouldn't the world be a better place if we all shared things, honey? If we used up what we have that's still good before we rush out to buy new?"

She even carries his old portable record player to her classes, one his grandparents gave him for Christmas when he was only a baby. She doesn't have time to drive to campus, she says, find parking, and pick up a pho-nograph—often broken anyway—then repeat the entire process to return it. Which seems to him no reason at all. No reason for an adult to carry a child's record player covered with red-and-yellow beach-ball stuff like wall-paper. Besides, she doesn't allow herself to "waste gas," since she teaches not on campus but in town, or else at the jail, or the army post or out at the air force base miles away. And "wasting gas," he knows it, really just means money again: *ochen dorogova*.

Darrin sighs, grits his teeth, squeezes his eyes shut for a minute before he stands up and walks towards her, and he's not dragging his backpack. He's being careful about that. They've already quarreled twice since he arrived from Juneau about him dragging things.

But why does she make him *feel* like dragging things? Even his feet? That's the real issue as far as he's concerned. *Why?* Why does *his* mother buy used coats that look nearly as bad as the one she's just worn out?

"Oh, honey," she says, seeing him at last, "give me a hand, will you? Grab these records before I drop them?" And one of her students—of course—rushes up to them from someplace. Popping out of the woodwork Dad would call it. "Here, Dr. Taylor, let me help." The student is hushed-voiced as they all are around his mother. Reverent, like somebody breathlessly saying a prayer they've worked hard to memorize.

So Darrin only grabs a few of the books, while the student—who has long dirty hair and a bad case of acne, as the hushed-voiced ones always seem to have, either or both—fumbles to take the records. Darrin hates it when they call her "Dr. Taylor." Because most of the time she stops right then, on the spot, to correct them. Blocking the path and in public, telling them her dissertation "isn't quite complete."

Not saying she can't afford to leave Fairbanks and go Outside to work on it, maybe never will be able to afford it, ever, which he knows is the truth. Saying only that she isn't really Dr. Taylor yet: *Just yet.* That's how she usually puts it: *Just yet.* The same when they say "professor." She's actually an adjunct faculty member she tells them, her voice so achingly precise. Not a professor: "Ms. Taylor will do fine."

He hates how she smiles when she says it, her face so damned pure. Glowing, almost radiant—*beatific*, he thinks that's the word; he came across it in one of her dictionaries. As if "being paid *nothing* to teach class after class, year after year," which he heard her sobbing about, crying into the phone to his grandmother one day last week, saying, "It's just—*wrong*, Mom. *Abusive.* So demeaning and hurtful." Well, smiling as if that's just what she's dreamed of, longed for forever while she talks with some student.

But she doesn't say any of it this time.

"Rodrigo, I'd like you to meet my son Darrin." She says that to the student instead. And Darrin nods politely, trying not to let his eyes wander over the student's strange-looking clothes and puzzling yellowish skin while his mind bounces the odd-sounding name like a basketball added to all the rest: Alaska Native? But what? Tlingit? Asian and African maybe? But then why

Rodrigo? Maybe Filipino? Surely not a Siberian? "Rodrigo is a chess player too, Darrin," she's saying.

Three freaks together, Darrin thinks. And he's suddenly ashamed of himself. Ashamed of his own clunky and uncontrolled mind—a racist's mind? His thoughts probably prove he's at least some kind of major snob-in-training. And snobs are what his mother hates most. He doesn't know how many times he's heard her proclaim it, thousands probably. And he *does* agree in a way. Totally maybe. But—face it—he does *not* want to be forced into playing chess with this head-bobbing person who reminds him of a bookend in his grandparents' bedroom in Juneau. Good God, no!

"Neat," he says instead, trying to smile at the student, hoping with a splash of her own phrasing to please his mother for once. Rodrigo smiles back painfully.

The bookend is what's left of a pair, Gramma's told him—a little ceramic man who looks like a pale Anglo version of an Oriental, a China boy thought up by a White man. The tiny ceramic head sways constantly, bobbing up and down anytime anybody gets anywhere near it. He can't imagine two of them, ever. He thinks somebody probably broke the other one to put it out of its misery—and now here's this real-life Rodrigo, still bobbing his head: *Three freaks together for sure!*

It's all too much. The kid from school. His mother studying Russian from the library's ancient records, even using his worn-out record player to play them. Then this student. Plus his tooth, aching all week. And how can he go to the dentist? He *can't* tell her about a stupid tooth: *will not*, since he knows she has no medical coverage and no money. He'll suffer in silence, Mom's son after all, and wait till next year with Dad when he'll be covered again.

And of course he won't tell her what he keeps thinking. He *won't*, dammit, will *not* tell her that he wants to go back to Dad. That he's homesick. That he'd rather be home in Juneau with Dad and his new family: *Home—* that's how he's begun to think of it.

No, he'll tough it out here, in the middle school he hates, no friends at all, avoiding bullies like a pathetic coward, a real freak. Watching TV alone most nights while she's out teaching. Trying to do homework in the tiny living room where she sleeps on the couch so he can have her bedroom. Listening to those scratchy records pouring out repetitive strange-sounding Russian phrases from the steamy kitchen, or to poets nobody ever heard of intoning long strings of pompous words. Riding in her worn-out Honda, hoping it won't break down or drift off on its bald tires into a snowbank.

Thinking about eating more than doing it since he knows how little money she has.

Thinking about being laid-back, cozy, sprawled in an easy chair in front of the big TV at Dad's, eating popcorn, staring into the fire, drinking pop or some delicious juice she calls "trendy" and refuses to buy, pigging out, joking with his stepbrother—*next year*. Being an ordinary American again, with parents who have real jobs that pay real money. Parents who let you buy new clothes rather than garage-sale specials. Who let you go to a movie rather than borrowing old ones—"classics"—from the library. Or to the dentist.

Because all that *is* what he wants, he sees it now. He wants to be free of the huge limping kid. To be a *real* American again, a snob, at Dad's. How can he tell her it's only October and already he'd rather be there? In Juneau with Dad and his new family?

Well, he *won't*, dammit. He's no quitter! He'll keep on doing what he's doing, just as she will. Walking stiffly ahead carrying borrowed books. Walking behind this weird-looking kid Rodrigo who's probably only one of hundreds she's teaching in required college English courses this semester for five dollars an hour.

He wants her to quit, to leave, to stop wearing her *KICK ME* sign. That's what he heard her say last week, a joke, to a fat woman, Barb, that she introduced in the hallway at her apartment building as "my colleague." He wants her to stop working so hard to keep alive some fantasy this abusive job seems to give her. He wants to be proud of her!

But she won't leave. He thinks she'll stay here forever, suffering silently, enduring her own version of all-powerful bullies, putting one foot in front of the other and smiling falsely, pretending not to be a snob, just like he's doing now.

But as soon as he thinks this, he knows he's wrong. She'll do something else entirely. She'll shame him in some new way he can't even imagine yet. So he says it again, slightly louder, to push that thought from his head: "Chess, huh? Neat."

Thaw

Fairbanks, January 1976:

In her sleep, Arlys heard the splash of meltwater dripping from the frost-covered bedroom window, and she swam toward the sound and entered it, her body curling and gliding inside it like a fish. But something moved away from her: a curved shape, almost familiar, it rose and turned, glowing, a face, almost a smile, its sinuous wake catching at her then slipping farther and farther away till that swaying motion crossed some far edge of sight and the creature lifted again, surfaced in the light, then sank into darkness. And she was awake, coughing, sitting up in a tangle of sheets that stank of cigarette smoke and sweat and the fish-smelling depths of her own body.

And semen? Could you smell semen? That faint, sad hint of salt—Bruce. *Tanax̂ Chuginadax̂ ayagax̂*—Christ!

She shook her head and pushed impatiently at the mass of tangled hair that lay damp and heavy against her neck: *Redhead*, that's what he'd said, wasn't it? What he'd called her, the kid: *a hot ol' redheaded gal*. Christ.

A puddle had formed on the worn hardwood floor, under the window, and the new quilt lay tossed aside so that one corner of its orange binding was soaking up water in a blood-colored splotch. In the big glass ashtray on the floor—Bruce's ashtray—among butt ends and ashes were bits and kernels of popcorn. Beside the ashtray, that tangle of crumpled red stripes. The paper sack that had held the drunk kid's popcorn. Her head throbbing now, pounding, and she reached to the nightstand for her wineglass—*two* long-stemmed glasses: *hair of the hound.* She downed the dregs from each.

Then it was true, all of it, every bit. At least he'd had the good sense to leave. Her forehead throbbing, hammering, she pulled the damp quilt from the floor to cover her bare chest, and felt her throat form again those strange words that echoed in the empty room: *"Tanax̂ Chuginadax̂ ayagax̂—"*

She stood up then, dragging the quilt across the damp floor to the window, and pressed her forehead to cold glass, wetting her skin, easing the throbbing. So damned if it wasn't a thaw: "An honest-to-God thaw, Bruce—*yes.*" It was a whisper. Then, louder: "Say that aloud too, *Bitch*, to no one. Why not? Go ahead," and she was laughing or coughing or both—

True, yes, everything, not just the kid. Sky imperial blue, the sun alive, the window glass shimmering in sudden heat. True that the warmth felt no more freakish than anything else, no more strange than Fairbanks swollen with Pipeline dollars: *Two Street* only a few blocks away but another world from what it was as Second Avenue. Newly rich workers back from the Slope everywhere, striding down *Two Street* in heavy boots and Carhartts, women lounging on corners and in doorways inviting them to party, no matter the cold. And none of this more strange in mid-January than yesterday's weird "normal," two weeks of minus fifty degrees when the bedroom wall was flocked with blue patches of frost, a five-o'clock shadow of frost, like the chin of a hungover Pipeliner.

Yesterday hoarfrost lay thick as a bleached Turkish towel shrouding the windowpane. At midnight last night: not nearly drunk enough as she dressed like a boom-town whore for the perpetual party downtown. But now her bare toes brushed something. Cold glass. She lifted the nearly empty wine bottle from the floor, closed her eyes to suck it dry.

Yesterday the sun was visible to her unshielded eyes. It hung all four hours of the illumined day like a neon moon skating across the horizon—a lipstick moon, a nectarine caught in that gauze of yellow fog. And the thick air, dangling its prize, swirled and fell like liqueur sliding into a crystal glass, air wicked as crème de menthe. Not merely fog, but thick and thin tangles of air. *Ice fog:* the mother of air, its skin, its bones, its unholy breast, pinkish or golden by turns, radiant sometimes then dingy and streaked, torn, gray, defrocked cloud. Transformed like her life, a mirror for the new world downtown, as she steadied herself, careful, bending to place the empty bottle back on the floor.

But a live bird soared at the window feeder as she stood. Coming from nowhere like everything else, it had misaimed and its small gray form thudded against the glass as if it might strike Arlys's throbbing head, her pale, sickly face, but the creature fell instead, pulsing, onto the window ledge. She gasped, stepped back to avoid the bottle and into the ashtray, her bare heel splintering popcorn, as the bird righted itself to pick at the few dark sunflower seeds left among damp bits of straw. The crest on its tiny head was an injury, another, dark red, lifting and dipping toward her as it fed: a wound fresh as her own, permanent, signaling injury to her again and again, shiny and damp with mockery.

Redpoll, she told herself, *redpoll*. Her favorite species of bird, and this lone poll the first to appear all winter. Unseasonal as the thaw, for they usually came in February, dense clouds of tiny birds: *bird wars*, chest-butting each other for seeds from the feeder.

And she saw Bruce—not the kid, not the shy young man with his Flame Lounge popcorn, but Bruce standing at the window in the old days, a cigarette dangling from his lips. His fair-skinned form was boyish, angular and too tall for the threadbare orange bathrobe. He rubbed at his blond chin then turned to grin at her, his narrow jawline widening with the grin as he watched other redpolls, long-gone generations of redpolls, whirling outside this very same window.

Her heart was a damned fish, flopping again, and she closed her eyes to say the words once more in the best guttural rendering of Aleut she could manage: *"Tanax̂ Chuginadax̂ ayagax̂ an̂ĝiisanax̂ ax̂takux̂*—our volcano breathed through a woman—"

Were redpolls really the same birds as the ones the Aleuts called rosy finches? Asiatic birds—Siberian finches?

But no. The drunken kid—no, no, the young man; she must grant him that, he was a man—he'd said no. How strange to think that this young man knew the legend as she did. Loved it too, maybe the single thing they could share purely. Arlys pulled a cigarette from the crumpled pack on the nightstand and lit it, flopping down on the bed to inhale while she stared at Bruce's old metal lighter, gleaming and cold in her hand, then dropped it onto the quilt. Her body felt strange: heavy, old, filled up with endless sorrow.

Twenty-three, he'd said he was, the kid. Twenty-three indeed. "Twenty-three skidoo?" she'd joked, his nice grin widening. And his name? Sylvester maybe? Shy Sly. Or Simon? Simple Simon, met on the way to the fair? With herself the old-lady-who-gives-good-head? At least he was not a Pipeliner.

"Christ, *Christ*," she whispered, "what have we come to, Bruce?"

But there was no "we" anymore, of course. She tossed the lighter onto the nightstand and gazed around her at the cluttered room: at her dropped boots and underwear, jeans draped on the chair, then at her own watercolor of New Brunswick, small and amateurish: the house she was born in pinned up beside the window. And she thought of Toronto, a real city, a city she loved; a magical place she'd moved to on her own, at nineteen. Then of how she'd come to Fairbanks, where she'd stayed—like a fool—ever since.

That was because of Bruce. His letters had bewitched her, alternating those lyrical descriptions of the sun at midnight or two a.m. with long help-less passages in which he swore he would kill himself:

It's much more than Dad or school or even learning to paint, Arlys. You know everything here, in this light. I see and know everything. I become more certain each day—don't laugh my dear—that I will never be an artist. And if you don't love me, if you won't have me, what good am I to anyone, principles or not, alive or dead?

Blackmail it seemed now. She'd taken her earnings as a supermarket checker—savings for her next semester at art school in Toronto, where they'd met: Bruce, the shyest American she'd ever known, the tallest, the poorest, the most talented and most naïve. The most beautiful, too. His long-fingered hands were like hypnotized dancers when he painted; how she'd loved to watch him paint, *had* watched till the end.

And she'd bought a car, the old Pontiac she still drove, on the occasions when she *did* drive anymore, was sober enough for it. Then, hoarding her parents' slack objections as if they might be well-disguised signs of love, she drove across North America. To Alaska. To Fairbanks. To Bruce.

"To save Bruce from himself," as she liked to think of it afterwards, savoring the joke, because she was surely no salvationist, and of course neither of them was "saved" in any sense at all. She crushed the cigarette and saw Bruce as he was that summer: still painting his wild, big, strangely delicate canvases when she arrived, indeed till the end; staying in school in Alaska with his grandmother's money, then hers, waitressing money. His letters already almost beside the point by the time she'd arrived to the light. That transformative subarctic light which she too loved at once, pulling into town in the Pontiac exhausted and broke, but also a bit ecstatic, two weeks after his last deathly letter.

And that was more than twenty years ago. Maybe more than the whole of the kid's life, the young man's. Years and years like the idle conversation of a Saturday, sitting in a booth at Co-Op Drug. Smoking, drinking coffee, relaxing after a morning of sex, cradled in the calm sleepy leisure of an ordinary subarctic winter before oil deformed the town.

They had never married. Twice Bruce had begged her, begged her for months to marry him. And once she'd agreed. But at the last moment she'd left him standing alone. Bruce framed by the dark wood of the hallway that led to the office of the justice of the peace. His back was to her, so calm and unsuspecting in his black leather jacket, each bend and dip of his back so familiar, so vulnerable.

He'd held a cigarette cupped low in his bare left hand, and the pale yellow hairs on the back of his hand curled like golden threads. *Medieval*, like a painted saint, not human at all, with no sense of the tragic core of life he embodied so deeply, so completely, while their marriage license dangled like a cobweb—yes, that was her reason: Medieval. His gentle face lit for a second by the cigarette's flare when he lifted it and inhaled, their license dangling in his other hand, so weblike and weirdly chilling beside the mated black gloves he clutched in his pale right hand.

She'd run, with tears streaming down her live healthy face. Yes, *run* then—the six blocks back to this very apartment. This same apartment that the two of them even then shared, each by that time formally, minimally, employees of the university.

And that had been—what? Fourteen years ago? Sixteen?

No, Arlys decided, fifteen. She lit another cigarette and inhaled slowly. The thought of marrying Bruce—gentle, good Bruce, that simple-hearted man she had always loved tenderly—*would* goddamned love always and ever and forever—*had* loved from the first moment she saw him in that corridor at the art school in Toronto—

Marrying Bruce had seemed an absurdity.

No, worse. Marriage to Bruce would be a violation, an unfair act she could not bring herself to commit. Or explain. But she'd tried. To explain that she loved him as she'd love no one else in her life. That she loved him with all her heart. (It was true.) But that it would be wrong—unforgivably wrong for exactly this reason, *love*—to marry him.

Bruce had never understood, of course, and that fact was all the more reason why she could not marry him. She crushed the new cigarette fiercely in the bedside seashell on the nightstand, an ashtray that had also, once, been a treasure belonging to Bruce, and rubbed at her forehead.

Last spring he'd married a nineteen-year-old girl, the least promising of his students in the fall watercolor class. Her name was Melonie. When Arlys saw the spelling of the girl's name on his class list lying on the hall table—which she saw in September, more than a year ago, long before she glimpsed the girl, perhaps even before he did—Arlys thought madly, suddenly, like a cartoon strip in her head, of the lush roundness of gourds, of melons, of fullness, curves, the tropics, the fertility and heat of the sun.

But Melonie was all angles. She was thin and sallow and silent, dressed always in black or navy blue, the oldest child of alcoholic parents, Iñupiat who lived in a tiny squalid house in downtown Fairbanks just a few blocks from this apartment. Yet, oddly, when she met the girl for the first time, at an art show on campus that fall, Arlys was shocked to see that she too liked her. Quiet, serious Melonie. Her dreaminess. Her soft honest glance, that openness, a gentle naïveté perhaps even greater than Bruce's, and the slow, clean way she gazed at him.

By the time Bruce moved out of the apartment in February last year, taking a room in a rundown communal house near the river shared by artist friends, and by Melonie, Arlys felt, to her own amazement, no jealousy: she herself was the one always pleading for openness in every relationship, wasn't she? How could she be jealous?

Nor in May, when she attended the wedding, that sad little joke of a wedding. She'd felt no jealousy at all. Only a feeling like fatalism. Or maybe sheer self-absorption. As if her own glance into the depths of that class list on the hall table had caused everything.

And a feeling like dying. A feeling like death itself creeping into her body to curl firm and thick as a fetus. Ordinary life began to pull away from her in May too, sliding and drifting away while she sank deeper and deeper into the need to drink—

And it was this sinking, she told herself now, combing shaky fingers through the matted bright hair drooping against her neck, *this* that she must not accept. It was this sinking, this weight, this mad doom that made her invite the young men—boys even, barely more than that—as if she herself were infested by Pipeline madness.

She rose quickly, pulling on her bathrobe and swearing to herself that she would not bathe. This young man, too, had brought life—had brought hope with his talk of the Aleut tale she loved, and she'd keep the life of his body for as long as she could.

But the bathrobe itself seemed a weight, and she sat again on the edge of the bed feeling doom. On the night of their wedding in May, Bruce and Melonie drove off in the long evening sunset toward Denali Park, for their honeymoon. No one had seen them alive again. Bruce's truck was in flames off the side of the road in a shallow canyon beyond Healy when it was found at two that morning.

In nightmares Arlys saw the scene as a blossoming, fierce and volcanic, the truck's fiery blooms paintlike and surreal in her mind, deadly weapons she'd somehow invoked. Heat and fire consuming everything she'd ever loved. But of course such egocentricity was at the heart of her problem. *My disease*, she thought. Exactly what she must reject.

The phone rang then, its jangling loud and real, separate from the smoke and flame of her sorry thoughts. Yet Arlys's faint, weak "Hello?" felt abstract, a whispered question.

"Umm—it's Silas. From last night?"

The disembodied slow voice was low-pitched, and a question, like her own. It hissed in her ear with its *Silas*. So he was *Silas*, his name a sibilant rhyme for her own.

"Did I maybe leave a parka?"

"A parka?" She looked, dragging the phone. No, not on the bedroom floor or the chair. The living room? Closet or hall table? Kitchen counter or floor? Desktop? No.

"No, Silas. No parka." And a female voice came through the receiver in the background, another question. A young Native woman's voice, full of emotion, but clear and palatal as Melonie's: "*—with that old lady?*"

Christ!

Then her own voice, calm, breathing against the receiver: "No, Silas, no parka."

Silence from Silas. Then: "Sorry to have bother—"

"No parka." Her hands, her whole body trembling, and the receiver back in its cradle.

These tears were hot and familiar. She sat on the edge of the bed reliving her fortieth birthday. It had come in October, a Saturday, five months to the day after the funeral. She'd wept for hours that day, wept stupidly as she tried—only that—to dress. But she could not dress, not move, so she'd stared at her body in the mirror: a flabby, pale, big, half-nude aging woman weeping, pretending to be abandoned.

Not really widowed but feeling that way, taunting Death by trying to peer into flesh. Pretending to be pregnant with nightmares and dreams. A sad and sorry joke.

And she'd finally begun to study each mole and sag, each swell and lump and faint discoloration of her skin as if she might yet find some answer. Some vast awful truth beyond the tired-out one she'd felt since she was nineteen—that her body was Bruce's possession. Not hers at all, but *his*— its weight and height, its healthy glow, even its voluptuousness, each was a puzzle to her, very nearly a burden, while Bruce had celebrated it.

Yes, her body had been his new land, his triumphant discovery far more than art or life in Alaska with that surfeit of darkness and light, the pure air he raved about. Her body was the dreamland he'd been impelled to, bringing his youth. He'd clung to her as he had to art school, staying on till they hired him to teach three classes each semester on campus. Her body had been his all, his world, his new land. Once—for a time.

Then she'd known suddenly, on that birthday Saturday, with a chill colder than any January, the terrible truth about sin: that not loving enough was the only real human sin, the worst possible evil in life. Maybe the only profound truth she'd ever discover.

And that was my mistake, my sin, she'd decided on that day. Not the refusal to marry or the three abortions, but a larger sin against life itself. A failure to love Bruce enough.

Her rejection of Bruce's love had brought all this grief—but maybe also its truth? And she'd understood that she wept because she wanted a child. Only a child. Not Bruce. Not the drinking that had already begun by then, but a child of her own blood and flesh. Only a child. A child she would love enough: *perfectly, completely—truly,* as she herself had not loved but been loved, once, by Bruce.

She started the series of paintings then, on that terrible birthday Saturday in October, and she knew at once what she must call the series: "Children of the Interior Valleys." They were more than an obsession or a penance. They were a groping back toward life, an action as necessary as breathing, and as simple.

And they were beautiful. Each of the child faces was simply and cogently beautiful, the best painting she'd done in a lifetime of amateurish dabbling and struggling. She could stand apart from each of them objectively, as she could from nothing else in her life, and say of it: "Yes. This is good."

Arlys loved each of the faces too, separately and deeply and purely. Each flat, sad, solemn face and each roundly absurd or generous one. Even the haunting ones that stared from the canvas with no expression at all. Each was itself, a beloved child to Arlys. But it was not enough. Her body began to ache that October for the young men. And mornings when she woke, there was often that mad tangle of thoughts lying just below the edge of consciousness—just as today. She knew that she must be hunting something in all these faces. A single face perhaps? The face of the child who would become her own child?

But of course all this was ridiculous. Obsessive. Absurd as the legend.

Sick, Arlys told herself, and she stood and spread the damp quilt on the bed with hands that would not stop trembling. She tossed the empty bottle into the trash and forced herself to take two Swiss cheese slices from the almost-empty refrigerator and chew while she dressed, chomping three aspirins with glugs of wine from the refrigerator between bites. To ease her throbbing head, which at last began to quiet.

And it was a new day. The ice fog had lifted completely. So she'd drive to the airport, yes, and catch a bush flight to a village. Today, on this clear gift of a day, she'd surely discover a new face.

She braided her red curls quickly and drew the black slash of eyeliner she thought of as whore's eyes, a dark Pipeline eye sketched on each eyelid with a practiced if unsteady hand. She pulled on clothes, and her skin in the mirror was soft and freckled, rosy as a child's or a farm wife's. "My Viking maiden," Bruce had called her—a joke about her health and fairness and height, and a bow to her reckless courage—and she grinned at her tall reflection. Well, a Viking it would be. Or a misplaced, miscolored, and wrongheaded Aleut sailing off in a bush plane toward some inevitable blood-rimmed dawn.

She stuffed pajamas, makeup, hairbrush, and toothbrush into her ready satchel, with a canvas and sketchpad and paints. Then she was whispering the words again as she closed the apartment door: *"Tanax̂ Chuginadax̂ ayagax̂ an͡giisanax̂ ax̂takux̂*—Mt. Cleveland—no, no, our *Chuginadax̂* breathed through a woman—"

Next summer she'd actually travel to the Aleutian Islands for herself. She'd see Mt. Cleveland, her own *Chuginadax̂*. And she'd pay for the trip with sales of her paintings, by God. For in late October, a week after her birthday, she'd quit the job at the university bookstore that she'd held for years, emptied her retirement account, and rented a downtown studio, on *Two Street* above the swaggering Pipeliners. And it was working out, by God, all on the strength of her sales.

Now she unplugged the engine heater, carelessly coiling the heavy cord on its hook on the Pontiac's front bumper. She and Silas had plugged it in last night, she remembered doing it—Silas a coastal kid, joking about it, eager for the exotic sight, a big ol' car with its long black umbilicus—and she bent to unlock the door. When she sat on the cracked upholstery and pumped the accelerator, she was shocked that the engine, miraculously, being cranked for the first time in weeks, turned over on the second good try.

For it seemed to Arlys that Bruce had left her, if nothing else—she could feel it—*luck*. There were the paintings for one thing, Bruce's legacy in some uncanny but very real sense, and she leaned back into the frosty stiffness of the old leather upholstery and whispered the words again: *"Tanax̂ Chuginadax̂ ayagax̂—"*

The legend too must be a gift from Bruce. Why else could she love it so? It was called "The Chuginadak Woman," and it told of a volcano woman and her quest for love. Arlys had discovered the tale only last August, at work, but it carried her across the wasteland of Bruce and Melonie's fiery death far more compassionately than painting or drink or sex—or even that repetitive and merciless truth about not loving enough.

She tapped the accelerator pedal lightly and imagined the smoky flesh of the volcano woman taking human form, crossing the Aleutian Chain to hunt for a husband: a man she'd seen only once, the man who could catch rosy finches in his bare hands. Then the woman—Arlys saw her: husky, strong, tan, striding purposefully—a mythic female who walked miles and miles until she finally found him: the man of her long dreaming.

It was her hug, an embrace—only that—which sent him, and her, headlong down the mountainside—exciting her, killing him. Arlys closed her eyes, feeling that embrace, then seeing the man's father, an Aleut chieftain, kill the woman in retaliation.

But the finest part came at the end, when the chief restored both lovers to life. He saw that the Chuginadak woman—in her grief now fully and truly human—*did* love his gentle son. That restoration to life always seemed perfect to Arlys, more hopeful and beautiful, with its acceptance of dark fate, than any European myth.

She sighed aloud, putting the car in gear. The tale somehow retold her own life too, the woman's fatal lusty weakness, like her own, rising from a crude and unconventional strength, that zest for living she could not cast off, even when it became destructive. Yet a strength that was oddly conventional in the end: heterosexual, loving, so clearly *female*. A *real* strength, and yet the source of her weakness—a riddle to frame her own being.

When Arlys backed across the black slushy ice of her parking spot, an assigned spot that was once the lawn of the apartment building, the Pontiac's wheels slid treacherously, and she grinned, thinking of the Chuginadak woman and of her own redpolls. Well, she was ready, truly ready, for any small new battle life might offer.

It was a beautiful day after all. Sunlight glinted off melting ice and snow everywhere, the sky a vastness of clear cerulean. And no Pipeliners in sight! They must be sleeping it off. There was a sweet, clean scent to the air, a pure tea-brewing smell Bruce would love. It hadn't been here for weeks, pouring now through the car window as she rolled it down. The Pontiac lurched across ice mounded on the sidewalk, edging toward the street, and Arlys felt that maybe things would begin to be right again. Even her head felt almost cured in this fresh air.

So maybe the quiet young man with his Flame Lounge popcorn—shy Silas with his lost parka—would become the last young man? Because he was an Aleut and knew the legend, he'd even told her that rosy finches were not the same birds as redpolls. And none of the others—not one—had ever heard any of it before.

Perhaps there was a pattern to life after all. For she'd loved Bruce as well as she could at the time—most fiercely, it seemed, when he—bold and unconventional at last—chose Melonie and they'd actually married.

And surely Bruce's love for her over all those years was all the love anyone could possibly need in a lifetime. And today was a day of thaw!

"Besides which, I'm a rich woman!" She whispered these last words aloud, thinking how strange—and how fine—it was to be paid for every painting! *Paid* for paintings you yourself loved so much that not even giving them up, accepting unthinkable amounts of money for them, even secondhand Pipeline dollars, could ruin them.

The Pontiac's bald tires bounced across the rutted slush and snow of Seventh Avenue, and Arlys imagined money—clean, new American dollar bills—swirling and falling on her. Dollar bills alighting like small birds to cover the dashboard of the car. Dollar bills draped on the milk-colored plastic shoulders of St. Christopher, the travelers' saint Bruce sent her more than twenty years ago—sending it as a joke, he'd said, "a hint," mailing it to her weeks before she decided, on that whim, to leave Toronto. Though she'd been sure at the time that it was a sincere gift: a passionate token of his love. Maybe even reverent, or at least sentimental—a rosy finch flying to her across North America long before she'd heard of such a bird.

Now she was counting exactly how much money she'd earned on the series. She closed her eyes for a second to calculate: nearly ten thousand dollars.

Ten thousand dollars, as the bald front tires lurched on and she reopened her eyes to the familiar rundown homes and businesses. The north corner with its log cabin realtor's office, a touristy gift shop, the music store with its back wall painted into a psychedelic swirl of piano keys—the mural so like a creature from her own mad dreams.

So maybe Bruce was right, and life was indeed good. For surely Bruce had brought her all this—this inevitable future, this new vision and its wild success. Maybe at last reversing what she felt for weeks after the wreck, and even at times now in fits of near madness: that she'd somehow parceled out his and Melonie's terrible end. Her fault.

For of course such things *do* happen in Alaska. Always have and will. Distance, cold, vastness, and weather each so endlessly potent. That was the sane fact. Alaska, as in the legend, was simply a vast, volcanic, and eternally volatile place. "No, no, *is*. Present tense, keep that in mind, old girl." She said it aloud, her head barely throbbing.

Arlys saw the child then. He was small and frail, an Athabascan boy about eight years old walking twenty feet or so ahead of the Pontiac, coming toward her on the sidewalk, near the street, carrying a yellow plastic lunchbox he swung in an awkward rhythm—

And his face—*Christ!* Even in the glare of sunlight on ice, Arlys knew that face. She could not make her eyes move away from that face—

She felt the Pontiac begin to skid, and she braked, hard, remembering as soon as she'd done it that this was the worst possible thing to do, a wrong instinct, another reason she now rode the bus all winter, her newly bad reflexes—and the car was skidding, rolling, and bouncing across the sidewalk heading straight for the child—

～

She could remember no thud, nothing else. But suddenly it must have been over. Done.

Arlys heard people running, saw them dimly through a blur in her eyes that had to be tears. She sat in the mounded slush and ice at the edge of the sidewalk holding the bloody child's body cradled against her chest.

But that thick, sobbing noise—it must be coming from her own mouth. And she pressed her mouth against the child's matted black hair. Not to quiet the noise at all but to share what was left of the child's earthly being—

So this is my own child. She thought it clearly, ignoring the incomprehensible rise and fall of human voices that was everywhere in the air. And she sobbed into the child's thick hair, feeling the seep of his blood warm against her breasts.

Then the people standing nearest to her feet were bending toward her. Their arms were moving, and their lips, and one of them was weeping. They were shaking their heads too, talking. And they were pulling her child from her arms—but why?

And Arlys heard the familiar sound of her own voice, her own voice as they held down her arms, pulling the child away.

"She's in shock." A man's voice said it, his heavy words pouring over her lighter ones like the splash of a waterfall drowning the soft steady drip of new rain: "She's in shock."

"*I love you.*" Yes, yes, it was her own voice, saying the beautiful words again and again to the child so softly, for all the world to hear: "*I love you.*"

The Immediate Jewel

Twila Broder watches her daughter's right foot: the long toes dappled with chipped blue paint like fingers on a nail-biting child's hand pressing down, fanning out, spreading across the sole of the flower-covered plastic sandal. Then Mary's snaky heel lifts and rises, moving away from the gas pedal—and the fingery toes push down again, bending, splaying out, each toe moving separately like somebody typing something on a keyboard, in harmony, on the brake pedal now. Size 11. Can Mary's flimsy sandals truly be size 11? Bigger than Twila's own huge feet?

"That's good," Twila says. "You're doing fine. A nice smooth stop."

"Should I go around in another circle?" Mary's voice is high-pitched and sweet.

Too sweet, Twila worries, a sound like flowers rustling in the breeze, a wild rose newly opened, wafting its heart out in the dense smoke-thickened air. It still puts knots in Twila's chest to think that Mary chose to live with her grandmother—not herself, not Charlie—two years ago during the divorce. Is bookish Mary destined to be somebody like Mom then? Sweet and stubborn, like her Gran? Twila sees her mother in the smoke-yellowed light of the kitchen this morning: lips pursed, plump hands clasped, so superficially unobtrusive. But in fact she's a hammer, boldly and willfully naïve, Twila thinks, a woman as maddeningly lacking in any but the most absolutely conventional opinions as it's possible for a human to be and still breathe air.

What there *is* of air, in this smokiest summer Twila's seen in a lifetime of summers in Alaska. Weeks of out-of-control forest fires have turned sunny Fairbanks into a miserable minor scene from Dante.

"You could head across the snow dump," Twila answers. "Towards that dirt road by the ball field." The snow dump, nearly melted now, is the dark remains of a mountain of dirty ice left from the winter's plowing of city streets. Twila imagines rather than sees it through the smoke, a hundred yards beyond the barely visible asphalt of the parking lot. Few other cars have ventured out this morning, though Twila can see the sun, visible and orange as a harvest moon through the smoke, then the hazy outline of a man in a white painter's mask walking a black lab along the bike trail bordering the Chena River.

It must be boring for the girl, Twila's thinking, to drive around in circles like this every Saturday morning and Monday and Wednesday evening of the entire smoky summer. But Twila's determined that Mary learn how to drive, *now*, while it's easy, rather than as a clinically depressed married adult, at nineteen, as she did. Yet her daughter shows so little authority—or *confidence,* maybe plain old interest or just basic engagement—that Twila hopes, pointlessly it seems during each agonizing session, that the sheer boredom of the route will spur something rebellious in the girl.

Twila's ashamed to admit it, even to herself, but she sometimes longs to reach across Mary's bare knees in the short denim skirt, grab the key from the ignition, pull her long, skinny colorless daughter out of the car and shake her, hoping to bring the girl to life in the wildfire-transformed air. Has her own lifelong combativeness somehow reduced Mary to a being who *folds* so damned easily? Does Mary simply care for nothing?

Or care nothing for me? Hate me for the divorce, maybe that? Twila wonders all this at once, and a knot seizes her chest again. They've been practicing driving in the paved lot behind the convention center, behind Carlson Center, in Twila's trusty Toyota pickup since the first of June, when she managed to get the girl to pull her nose out of a book long enough to sign up for a learner's permit. But Mary seems no more in command this July Saturday than she was on that first sunny morning long before the smoke arrived.

"How'd things go for you and Gran this week in all the smoke?" Twila coughs a bit, rubbing her eyelids, her smoke-stung eyes, while Mary wends her way through another wide circle. Maybe in preparation for the eventful big right turn toward the ball field.

"Fine," says Mary. Ubiquitous *fine*. Always the girl's answer to any question.

"Your father might take a transfer to Anchorage." Twila hates to bring up that sore subject, but a nagging, unsentimental voice in her head insists: *Talk*. "Has he told you?"

"Yeah. He says I could spend parts of the summer, maybe some holidays, with him. Maybe my birthday."

Mary won't be sixteen till the twenty-ninth day of December, a day seared into Twila's head like the blizzard-wracked near disaster it was. In 1988, Twila a brand-new, very pregnant driver driving herself across town in Charlie's half-frozen truck with her knees clenched, her midsection throbbing in twelve-minute spasms. Then, when he'd left work and caught a ride to the hospital, Charlie's absolute unsteadiness. Which she'd known about always, of course, since the first day they met—in fourth grade. Though probably, sorry as the fact may be, his feckless quality must have been what attracted her: such a cordial, sloppy, reckless, and joke-filled boy. A bad boy. Charlie Broder made such vivid contrast to her own dull, dutiful, boring life. Well, after they'd signed her in at the hospital in the very last stages of labor, Charlie'd gone off and drunk himself into a truly horrible state. Thoroughly messy, though not an unfamiliar condition. He was not there for Mary's birth.

He'd actually left her alone, at the fancy new hospital where they'd both felt more than a little intimidated. Nineteen, each of them, and not even walking through the front doors confidently, as they might have into the old two-story wooden downtown haven of a hospital if it still existed—a place Twila still thinks of with real love.

And smoldering hate too: in her mind only, of course, since the building's now a bank. The *real* hospital, just off the banks of the Chena, a few miles upstream from the Carlson Center parking lot. The *real* hospital, where Mom worked away half her life, walking to work from their Slaterville house every morning at five. The old hospital, where she and Charlie were both born, only one week apart. Although of course she hadn't known that fact back then. Not till years into their friendship—or palship or courtship or dateship or sex life or huge mistake, whatever the heck somebody foolish enough to examine the thing might call it. What a flop their marriage had been! Amazing it lasted fourteen years.

Her own fault, of course. She *never* should've married Charlie Broder. In love or not, whatever that meant. Three months pregnant with Mary or not. She should never have married Charlie knowing as she had even at nineteen that her ambitions were already ten times larger than his ever would be. Knowing he'd happily—*proudly*—work a lifetime for the Alaska Railroad just like his dad. Barely sober most days. An engineer-in-training, then the real thing. A yard man, running flat cars and switch engines and oil tank cars, empty or full, from the train yard to the refinery every day of his life.

All day long, eight hours a day, the male version of Mom, in a way. Warmhearted and "a good provider"—a big, handsome, decent-enough guy, and the most fun on a sled or a snowmachine of anybody, but never really *there*. Drunk every time anything halfway demanding came along.

"He can get a railroad pass for me anytime. Whenever I want to visit, Dad says."

Mary's voice is a cupful of lukewarm water—reality—pouring slowly into Twila's head, while her daughter pulls even more slowly through the latest wide circle on their tiny map, but veering a bit towards the snow dump.

"You know I'm pretty well settled now," Twila answers. Not an answer at all: she knows it, and Mary knows it. "You could move in with me. It might be fun living so close to campus. With me instead of Gran, I mean. You know I'd be glad to have you." Is *glad* the right word? Is it strong enough? What did she practice? *Thrilled* would sound fake to Mary, and *love* feels like a painful irony these days.

There's silence in the car, just what Twila expects. Last fall Twila wangled herself down from full-time into a thirty-four-hour-a-week job at the meat-packing plant where she's worked as a bookkeeper since she finished high school. She's renting a roomy, inexpensive apartment near campus, taking a full load of courses. Psychology—and, of course, her mother thinks she's insane. A grown woman among hordes of pot smokers and reckless drinkers-and-drivers, teenagers and twentysomethings eager to throw away their lives. And what will she *do*, for godsakes, with a fancy degree in mind games? Not even teaching or nursing or computers-for-business, three things

Mom might understand and approve, *if* a person *had* to take up anything as senseless and overpriced as college.

Twila's mother herself worked most of her life, sweetly, as a nurse's aide. Until her knees gave out and the doctor insisted she "try something less strenuous," as Mom put it at the time. She'd worked two more years at a local drugstore, then found out, at fifty-nine, five years ago, that she could live pretty much as always—poor but comfy—without working, supporting herself on a small disability check added to Dad's post office pension. She's even managed to keep the house—its mortgage paid off ten years back.

Twila's mom now spends most days puttering around the house or the yard on her rebuilt hip and knees, home-perming her fading red hair, driving her ancient pale-blue Buick that was Dad's pride and joy—with its tattered *BUSH-CHENEY 2000* bumper sticker that makes Twila nauseous. Visiting her "girlfriends"—women as plump and prematurely old as herself. Or running errands with her obese miniature collie—buying groceries and snacks for herself and the dog and Mary. Picking Mary up after school on days Mom regards as too cold for her beautiful, giant-size, skinny-as-a-rail, flaxen-haired goddess-in-training of a granddaughter to walk the ten blocks "home," since Mary doesn't like taking the school bus.

"You could stay in school at Lathrop. You wouldn't have to switch to West Valley." Twila says that. "Unless you want to, of course. Then you could switch. For the sake of variety or something. I could drive you to school in the morning before work—or you could take the city bus. That might be fun. You could visit Gran whenever you want. Your Dad too. Or Grandpa Broder. And before long maybe you'll have your license and you can use the truck. You wouldn't have to change schools."

Twila's surprised how convincing and objective—how controlled—her voice is. Not pleading as she'd feared, practicing for this moment for weeks, planning it word by word. All summer so far, even before the god-awful smoke settled in. "You could move in next week. Or in August maybe. To have time to make yourself at home before school starts. Living with me might give you a taste of what life will be like in college."

Will! Ha! I actually said will, Twila's thinking. That seed planted!

"Remember that sled Dad got us one Christmas?" Mary's wavery soprano suddenly asks that. *Why?* Twila wonders, watching smoky orange light pool on the dashboard.

"Oh, God," says Twila. "Yes. That toboggan. Actually—wasn't it a toboggan?" She can see the thing in the smoky air: rugged and well used, as long as a hearse. Charlie turned it up someplace and repaired it, secretly, so proudly, at the shop at work. A family gift, he said. *"Split Second Survival,"* Twila says aloud. The motto Charlie painted on the thing. Mary was seven or eight, her big front teeth still coming in. Twila sees it all clearly, like a photo that must exist somewhere: Mary beside the Christmas tree—gentle Mary, who even then loved only books—holding their cat Silky, now long dead, posing astride her new, terrible king-size sled.

"We tried it out on that big hill up on campus," Mary says. "I got a bloody nose when we crashed." They're both silent for a second, then Mary speaks. "Why did we use it only a few times, Mom? Remember how hurt Dad was that it didn't work out?"

"Well—we don't all enjoy the same things, do we? People—are *different*, right?" Why does Twila feel as if she's lecturing herself with these simple-minded, pat phrases?

"But I *did* love that sled," Mary says. "It was Dad's special gift. *Split Second Survival*. I still love the name Dad gave it." There's silence in the car, then Mary's soft voice: "'Who steals my fortune steals nothing. Who steals my good name steals'—how does the rest of it go, Mom?"

"Othello," Twila answers. "Isn't it *Othello*?" She feels as lost in this conversation as the two of them seem in the truck, circling the snow dump in impenetrable smoke.

Mary's nodding, braking carefully: "I've been reading it all week in an old book Gran has."

Roger's book. Twila shivers through a chill to think that. She too loves Shakespeare, and she *does* know bits of the plays. But then why should that fact seem strange? She chose psychology for exactly the reason Shakespeare must have chosen the stage: to seek truth. To try to understand this baffling world and one's own place inside it.

"Shakespeare's being ironic, isn't he?" Twila says, hoping to bring things back down to earth. "Right? Iago's tricking Othello, pretending to be his friend. Isn't the rest of it something like, 'Good name in man and woman, dear my lord, is the immediate jewel of their souls.' You probably know it a lot better than I do: 'Who steals my purse steals trash. 'Tis something, nothing. 'Twas mine, 'tis his, and has been slave to thousands—'"

"*Slave to thousands.*" Mary repeats the phrase solemnly. Fervently, slowly, almost a whisper, like somebody talking in her sleep. Her pale nail-polish-free hands are pressed tight to the steering wheel. The small truck barely moves. "How did you learn it, Mom?"

"Your Uncle Roger," Twila says. "That must be his book you're reading. Oh, Mary, I wish you'd had a chance to know him. He was such an amazing person. I think your Uncle Roger—I think he had a role in every play Lathrop High School performed when he was in school. He loved *Othello.* How does the rest of it go? 'But'—something—'but he that filches from me my good name robs me of that which not enriches him and makes me poor indeed.' Does that sound right? Your Uncle Roger used to recite that stuff over corn-flakes at breakfast. Oh, Mary, I'm so pleased that you're reading Shakespeare."

Mary's nodding. "Shakespeare's not easy," she says, and Twila's thinking that her own life must have gone off track when Roger died. She was exactly Mary's current age. Fifteen. Roger's death must have thrown her awry. Right into her wild friend Charlie Broder's comforting arms. Odd to see that clearly—*here*—all at once. A sad revelation in the smoke, but it must be true. Odd, too, to think that your brother, only two years older than you, might have been a better parent to you than the real parents you shared.

And maybe she *is* being too hard on Charlie. He certainly has every right to be who he is. Just as she does. Twila knows that's what Roger would say. Was she always too hard on Charlie? On everybody, still? Even on herself, maybe?

"It means you have to be true to yourself, doesn't it, Mom?" Mary sighs. "That's what Shakespeare really meant. Othello should've trusted Desdemona, right? He should have trusted his heart, not listened to Iago. A person is more than—her reputation."

There's silence in the car, then Mary's sweet voice again: "Aren't we lucky to live here? Not many towns have Shakespeare theaters. I loved *A Winter's Tale* in June. Isn't it great to sit in the dog mushers' field watching Shakespeare? Even Gran loved it."

Twila, who often hates Fairbanks, nods, not speaking, thinking of Roger. What a loss.

To die in a car wreck at seventeen. And what would he want her to do? *Now. Today.* What would Roger want for her—and for Mary? How should she be raising this baffling daughter? This complicated, fine, beautiful daughter who *does* have her own passions after all—Roger's niece? His death is one reason she's determined that Mary learn how to drive, of course. And drive well. But what about the rest of their lives?

"Maybe Anya and I will join the Groundlings next summer," Mary says, speaking of the troupe of teenage actors who performed *Macbeth* in June, staging their first play.

"That's a great idea!" Twila feels the day turning, becoming a rare gift. A window into her daughter's being, even her soul, through the smoke. "But who's this—*Anya?*"

"She's new. At school. Her parents are Russians. From Delta Junction. Isn't it lucky they put on the plays early, before all the fires began? It'd be pretty weird sitting out in the bleachers choking, trying to enjoy Shakespeare in the smoke." Mary's steering the small truck slowly across the field. "It's global warming, isn't it?" she asks softly, squinting, her pale lashes fluttering. Twila sees a wobbly line of cranes, barely visible, navigating the yellow sky. "The wildfires, I mean? All this smoke?" Mary's voice has a rich vibrato Twila hasn't noticed before. A beautiful voice. Nearly a woman's voice.

"Maybe so," Twila says. "Sad to say, yes. I suspect it is." Twila's now thinking of last summer, all that smoke drifting across the North Pacific from fires in Siberia.

"Gran doesn't believe in it. Global warming, I mean. Climate change."

"Well, your grandmother isn't always—she isn't the quickest person in the world to accept changes, I guess." Twila's voice has dwindled at the end. Because maybe that's actually it? The tie that binds? The trait that runs like a fatal flaw through this entire so-called family? Accepting change badly. But she suddenly feels as if Mary's thinking exactly the same thing—maybe Mary even thought it first. Planted the maddening notion in her head.

Mary laughs softly as billows of dust from the truck rise above the melted and dried-up snow dump to mingle with the smoke filling the field and the sky, filling the world for miles up, miles and miles in every direction of earth and sky. Six million acres of burning trees, smoke clouds the size of Texas, the newspaper said this morning, centered above the vast, surreal transformed Alaska they've created. *Smoke*: its awful smell like a campfire gone global. Inside the car, in the apartment, in her mother's house—everywhere.

Yet Twila's thinking that this smoke feels familiar. Maybe like ice fog in winter. Even the eerie mood it creates, that cloying, enclosed, trapped feeling, the mind-altering absolute foreignness ice fog imparts to every bit of the known world. Shape-shifter smoke—and fog. She can no longer make out the turquoise siding that colors the walls of the Carlson Center, vanished behind them in thick gray smoke.

"She says that Sergi—," Mary begins the sentence then stops to laugh softly, touching her lips with the fingertips of her long left hand. "I feel so disloyal telling you this, Mom. Because I do love Gran." Sergi is Twila's mother's fat arthritic twelve-year-old collie—and Mary's laughing harder, helplessly: "Gran says Sergi was her paramour in another life. Has she ever told you that? They were both minor members of the Russian royal family. Gran says she's absolutely certain about it. Sergi loves beef stroganoff."

Twila's laughing now too, both of them giggling helplessly—laughing their heads off together like fools, Mary honking the tinny horn of the truck. Two flat loud *beeps*, then a third one while they circle slowly, with every window up to keep out the smoke.

"But I wonder why—if he had so much power *then*, I mean—*why*," Mary asks.

"*Why* would Sergi reduce himself to what he accepts now? For love? Do you think?"

Twila's eyes well up with tears, though that's ridiculous. How proud she is of Mary—what a miracle to be the parent of such a fine and intelligent daughter, what a gift to share love with this sensitive being! And how she misses Roger. But she's laughing too, patting at her daughter's cool, pale, beautiful right knee, moving forward with Mary into what Twila suddenly sees is her own life, her real life: "Does she really say that?"

"She does," says Mary. "Yep. And Mom, I think believing all that—well, anybody who believes all that, *that's* somebody who can accept *major* changes."

Mary pulls slowly away from the snow dump, out onto the dirt road that circles the ball field, turning right in the thickening smoke. Twila, rubbing at hot tears, finds herself wondering when the air will be clear again. Normal enough for Midnight Sun Baseball. Breathing this stuff while you round the bases—or swing a bat or throw a ball, or even stand up to yell—could definitely do serious damage to even the healthiest lungs.

And that's the other thing about this smoke. It reduces you, cuts you down to size. Tries to put you on its terms absolutely, as life often seems to do, forcing you to submit. Tries to make you feel unable, under its sway, to live. To be anything but a gasping fish out of water, unable to breathe—even knowing you *must* breathe and you *will*. Like a marriage gone all wrong. But maybe it's mistaken—maybe the smoke has it wrong. People *do* have choices. You don't really have to submit.

"Maybe you're right," Twila says. "Your Gran may be more flexible than I give her credit for." Truth too, she's thinking, or living a life. More complicated—and far better.

"Dad too," Mary says. "I think Anchorage might be good for him. I think Dad needs a change in his life, don't you? I don't want to move in till next month, though. Not till after Gran's birthday. And I want to stay in my classes at Lathrop."

Twila rubs at her eyes again. "Oh, God," she says. "That's right. I totally forgot about your Gran's birthday. Next week, isn't it? July thirtieth."

Mary's nodding. "Anya's a leapling," she says. "It means she was born on February twenty-ninth—born in 1988, like me. She's sixteen, but she's only had four real birthdays. Isn't that pretty amazing?"

Twila's nodding. "It is. Amazing. I'd like to meet her."

"You'll like her. Anya loves Shakespeare too. But she's lucky. She's short."

Mary pauses, then says: "Mom, do you think the world can accept a six-foot-three woman? Or six-foot-four? Or not?" Mary's beautiful long hands seem expert on the steering wheel as she hunches forward, peering through the windshield, trying to see the turns in the dirt road bordering the barely visible field in all the smoke and dust. "Be honest," she says. "Tell me the truth."

Blizzard

That papery wisp of a voice comes first, then the glide and thump of slippers on the worn carpet of the stairs leading up to the front hallway. "Now this one," says the voice. It's barely audible, but those are the words, Myra's certain: "And this one."

Myra can see more than hear the individual gnarled fingers of that long left hand, the bony flat palm lifting and sliding, pushing against the wall as her mother-in-law ascends—she'd swear to it. And the hall door creaks on its hinges, the slippers thump softly and glide forward in the darkness like snowshoes—it's a wonder she's pulled on her slippers this time, Myra tells herself—and the reedy voice whispers again, closer, more distinct: "Yes, there she is. Asleep. She's asleep. Sleeping. Yes, she's asleep." Myra, who's become good at it, keeps her eyelids shut tight and does not move.

"Well, she's asleep," says the quavery voice, suspirant, not quite a sigh, and Myra's trying hard not to breathe: *that old-lady smell—is it real or imagined? Should I sit up? No!* Then the slippers, and the voice, change directions in the dark and begin the return trip, the descent back down the unlit staircase to the big bedroom Myra's daughter Rose turned over four summers ago, with no hesitation, to her Gram. Rose moved her own things into the tiny, slant-roofed guest bedroom under the stairwell till she went off to college—two long winters ago. Outside, the Lower 48, on a scholarship to the university in Seattle.

I should worry about the darkness, Myra tells herself. But her mother-in-law's mind seems pared down to something like an essential sixth sense: ordinary dangers elude Wina, even on the rare occasions when she wanders away. Frank's mother wears her body like a battered shield now, Myra decides, sidling carefully forth at that oddly protective angle inside it in some final round of self-preservation.

"Yes, *self*, damn her. Her or me." Myra hisses it, then sighs at her own mean-spirited assessment and tosses off the afghan to sit up. She's wide awake, rubbing at her cold upper arms, hearing singsong words like a school-yard taunt: *Dr. Myra Lawrence sleeps on the couch.*

It's how she often comes awake after teaching, Wina or not: curled up with a book, cold, on the living room couch, narrating her own maddening life. A wet spring snow, a real blizzard, blew in from Siberia during her Tuesday evening class—471, The History of Russian-Alaskan Contact. Fierce snow sent like a joke to enfold that grim history; not just Russian *matryoshkee* to match her own life, but long generations of troubles nested like dolls.

By the time she'd talked with three students, changed books for Wednesday—201, Western Civ—and put things away in her tiny four-person office, she was bleary-eyed. But, *lucky*—yes, she knew it—lucky even to have a job these days. The night-school person, in an office thanks to the kindness of tenure-track people with real jobs. So why couldn't she feel lucky?

She'd pulled on parka and boots, warmed up the snowy car, then dug and backed off campus to the highway for the half-hour drive from hell. Climbing into bed at 11:15 with Frank, who'd rolled onto his side snorting when she opened their bedroom door, seemed—as usual, and to quote Frank's grunts when she tried—"not a viable option." At five a.m., only half-awake in the cold living room, she's plumped the pillow again, pulled the afghan over her ears and was trying to decide if there might ever have been a perfect man for her. A working-class man like her father, maybe? Probably not Karl at all, she'd decided, and certainly not Frank—when she heard it: Wina, Wina. Myra tries, often, to describe such events to Frank, including her own increasingly bitter reactions. But her husband scoffs—less at the notion of his mother as innately selfish, Myra thinks, than at the possibility that any human ability at all remains, speech included, miraculously sheltered in that bent husk of Edwina's diminished and wizened form. She's less his mother to Frank now than some maddeningly painful and incomplete ruination. Still, it's true that only Wina's voice, even in this ghostly version, remains anything like her old self. And of course Frank rarely hears that. Myra admits it. Wina no longer speaks by day, except, in whispers, to the TV screen. Or to her own blurred image in the light-catching mirror on the north wall in the living room, offering up her piti-ful stacks of carefully folded Kleenex. Or her hands, her wrists: "Would you like these?"

Edwina Simmons Lawrence was as lovely as Rose once. Myra lies back on the couch to consider this, sighing and fingering the afghan, trying to make her heart stop thumping so damned hard. Or at least very attractive—she prefers that version. Yes, Wina was full-busted and stylish—like Rose—when Myra first met her. Nearly thirty years ago, impossible to believe all that! But—yes, beautiful. And Myra sees a sudden vision of Edwina at their wed-ding, hers and Frank's: Wina so gorgeous in that peach-colored spring suit. How could a fifty-year-old woman manage to outshine a twenty-two-year-old bride? And why is she smiling now at that once-bitter memory?

Because that's how she'd felt at the time. Outshone. Plain, intelligent Myra trying not to look at her new mother-in-law. Odd to remember it now, but yes, lovely was the only word for Edwina back then. Except for that haughty stance, the characteristic upthrust of her shoulders, which—thank-fully, maybe—spoiled the effect for Myra. Yet Wina was not haughty in fact, just witty and full of self-doubt, traits she tried hard to hide. She was bright and generous, very loving—Myra learned all that slowly. Wina had taught school for forty-eight years, starting off at sixteen in a one-room school-house, and the gestures were part of a carefully cobbled together plan: *class-room demeanor*. Armor again, Myra thinks, sighing.

Wina's told Myra how terrified she was to step into a classroom, some students a head taller than she was: big farm boys who hated school. Myra shakes her head, recalls how scary it was to begin teaching adults at forty-one, and she smooths the edges of the afghan imagining Edwina at sixteen, her first year: jumping rope in the schoolyard with her students, crying her-self to sleep at night out of sheer loneliness—for her sister, brother, and wid-owed mother, miles away. Wina was not rehired at the end of the year: she was a good teacher, the head of the school board told her, but she played too long with the children at recess. *Life*, Myra thinks, *what a tangle of sorrows and jokes!*

When Frank, Wina's only child, first asked Myra to consider selling his mother's condo in Chicago to bring her here to live with them in Anchorage—well, much as Myra longed to refuse, there seemed no other choice. Not after the diagnosis.

Alzheimer's. Edwina could no longer care for herself, but she was not yet ready for a nursing home. Too confused to understand any part of it, Wina at first resisted the move. Then—to Myra's continuing amazement—she cast all her sympathies with Myra, not Frank, as soon as she set foot in the house.

Once, after an especially vicious and yet typical-enough husband-and-wife quarrel—*not a lovers' quarrel at all*, Myra thinks, nearly angry again, remembering. *Were Frank and I ever lovers? Chained combatants maybe, or a yoked pair of worn-out oxen.* Even Edwina's arrival seemed like just one more increment in that endless cycle of work and worry and fault-finding that surely defined their marriage. Well, that time anyway—maybe four years ago—Myra had gone to Edwina afterwards and told her she was leaving Frank. Today, maybe. The kids were almost grown, Rose eighteen and the boys—the twins—fifteen. She'd finally get a divorce, she was that fed up. But Wina must not blame herself in any way—Myra was careful to try to explain that—the divorce would have nothing to do with Edwina. Not with her illness or her presence in their life.

Wina had said, "I know, I know. You must have your own life, Myra. I've divorced two men for exactly that reason." Myra laughs softly, remembering: Wina—still in her bathrobe, regal-looking in the burgundy-colored robe, clearheaded for the moment, very cheerful, and—typical—so generous, mouthing exactly those words.

Myra had not left, of course. Giving up was not her style. As witness herself sitting up now, alternately shivering and smiling on the couch, remembering life for Edwina. Her self-assigned role these days? Worrying over Edwina. And over Rose. Yes, Rose, Rose, like a sore tooth in her mind.

The furnace comes on, creaks, and Myra's mind shifts with the sound. To the birthday package she must wrap and get into the mail: *Today. Can we afford to enclose a check?* For the twins, freshmen in Fairbanks. Nineteen years old in a few days! On their own for the first time and doing well, decent grades, and she and Frank still managing to afford dorm fees and tuition despite the hopeless economy. *But where have the years gone?* And she sinks back against the pillow, rubbing at her forearms again.

This was the hour, once, that she'd saved for Karl. They'd never been lovers, never really had "an affair," maybe not even "a relationship," as her students might phrase it. No, maybe neither—to choose two likely and similar soap-opera terms Myra hates. She's a person made for commitment, she supposes, sighing again. Surely she and Frank, difficult though it's been from day one, have lasted through twenty-six years so far of this hopelessly complicated marriage mostly by dint of commitment.

And happily often. Another strange fact, but true. They've often been happy. Anyway, flings of any sort seem trivial to Myra, silly and pointless. Except of course for these flights of the mind that are so inescapable, yet so essential. Think, think, think. Ridiculous maybe. Frank says so. But then, don't people lead such thoughtless-seeming, trouble-filled lives because they don't know how to think? Can't be bothered to think ahead? She tosses off the afghan, stands, and picks up her cell phone from the end table.

It's the terrifying thing about Rose's life in Seattle these days. So thoughtless-seeming—*a love triangle?* But she must not let herself begin all that. *No,* Myra decides—or she'll never be able to teach tomorrow, and she pokes at the phone: *But. Too early? Only 5:00 in Seattle.* And she stops poking. *Anyway, I need my sleep to teach tomorrow: Today, that is. Tonight. Western Civ,* and she tosses aside the phone and lies down.

But maybe there was a triangle in her own life once—*Was that what it was?* Beyond herself and Wina and Frank? Karl was her colleague at the university back then, a foreign language professor, teaching German and Russian. Seven years ago, like yesterday.

He was divorced, as unhappy as she was, rearing his two young sons alone because his former wife needed her own space, her own life. Which she'd gone off to lead—not quite alone, Karl hinted. First in Canada, then in California and Mexico. They'd never been lovers exactly, she and Karl, though the feelings between them—she believes this still, always will, probably—were passionate and enduring, a shared form of love.

Mostly they'd talked, endlessly, earnestly—*passionately*—about the humanities and teaching. About students and their lives, or life itself. Rarely about themselves. In her tiny shared office before a class or, more often, in his—since Karl had tenure and a real office. On and on, talking and talking. Sometimes they'd had coffee together: paper cups of latte he'd deliver to her hands steaming hot, wonderful smelling. Pathetic? Maybe so.

But she'd loved him. Deeply, purely, strange as it seems now. Always an insomniac, a light sleeper and early riser her whole life, she'd saved mornings for Karl in those days. For thoughts of him. Like a daily meditation, nearly a prayer, mental pushups for the life of a person she loved: sending forth her wish that Karl's life would be—but *what?*

Fine, Myra supposes, *even without me.* Full and happy, meaningful as it should be. That's all it amounted to. But how odd.

Until Karl moved south to take a teaching position in Idaho. Wina had arrived shortly after, and Myra in truth rarely thought about Karl after that. No time, no energy, with Wina and family duties and her own studies. And *teaching*: part-timers have to work so much harder! And with so little to show for it! It's so damned unfair! But—with her own middle age advancing steadily too—and Frank's. And of course with the twins to worry over, and Rose—boys from school already sniffing after lovely Rose by then—well, there'd simply been no energy left to devote to Karl anymore, not even in her thoughts.

But, yes, a triangle must have been what it was. Like Rose. Only twenty-two and "in love." With a married professor! How could that be? How could it have happened? That's what she's asked Rose, over and over, and received no answer. Is Rose a "home-wrecker" then? But—no. He's separated, alone for nearly a year.

"He has a child, Rose," Myra said on the phone last week. "Think of that, please. Think of her."

"Lots of people have children, Mother. Having children doesn't absolve a person from the human race." That's what Rose answered! Like a foot race, Myra thought—a damned foot race! Rose, Rose! Maybe she and Frank somehow damaged the girl with all their ridiculous quarrels? With this pitiful excuse for a marriage? Will Rose go through life unable to love appropriately?

But then, what is "appropriate love" after all? Myra picks up the phone again and pokes at it, thinking that: Can anybody love merely appropriately?

Is it possible? Could such a vast emotion ever be so narrowly circumscribed? And should it be? *Of course not*—and she tosses the phone down again, onto the end table: *I can't text. Should I write a letter? No! Besides, Rose is no longer a child. Respect her age and intelligence.* Myra lectures herself with that now: *And try not to focus so much on her sexuality.* Her physical being, her lovely body—plunging her into womanhood at twelve. So like Wina in that. Rose probably inherited Edwina's gorgeous complexion too, Myra decides: creamy skin, strawberry blonde hair, and that bustline—which men simply cannot resist.

But she's also intelligent. Myra admits it: Rose's mind so very like Edwina's once purely factual one, that calm and bold practicality. So like Edwina, once: maybe Rose will think her way through? Or is Rose's mind actually more akin to Myra's own complicated and drifting one? This nearly useless-seeming, wandering intellect. Not a historian's mind at all, probably. Rose, gifted or cursed with this same strange mind? "Mom's sifty-sorty, East-meets-West mind," as Rose used to joke, when she was fourteen or so. Wasn't that what Rose called it: "Sifty-sorty? East-meets-West?"

And this so-called professor—an adjunct only, like herself. Another part-timer. No future to speak of. Probably thinking "love" must be what he lacks, rather than a real job, academic fairness and equity! Well—he must be to blame. He's twenty-seven, an adult after all—and a professional! He must not be allowed to prey on a student. On Rose!

I'll phone a dean in Seattle to register a formal complaint. She thought it yet again, picking up the phone then putting it back down: Rose would be furious at that. And suppose everything just blew over. Began to seem tiresome and stupid, silly all at once to both of them. Not love after all. That could happen. In a way it seemed quite possible—yes, very likely. Maybe Rose would come to her senses.

She and Frank had tried to instill decent values. They'd stuck to their own marriage—and not just for the kids' sake, though they thought of that. And Rose is surely a good person. Kind and affectionate, intelligent, brave. Responsible too, Myra decides—she's always been so responsible, and very hard-working—just like Frank and herself.

Maybe it's Alaska. Could raising Rose here be to blame? Such a free-spirited place, and at such a remove from their families. But—no. Coming to Alaska was the best part of their life as a family, certainly the central event in Myra's own life. She recalls the smell of the boreal forest as they drove the highway north through Canada that first time. Like coming home—or like falling in love. The Chugach Mountains, the slant of daylight that first summer, almost no darkness at all. And the North Pacific. Whales spouting in Cook Inlet, and that ever-changing curve of rocky coastline. How could any of that possibly harm anyone? Surely such a world could only make Rose stronger.

So where did they go wrong? Where have they failed? And Frank—so typical!—he simply refused to talk about it. *Refused.* Not another word. That's what he said on Sunday evening: "She's an adult now, by God, we have problems of our own, Seattle's a long way off, and we know too damned little. Now, not another word."

But of course a person *needs* to talk. Talk is life in a way, isn't it, for people?

And before Myra has time to think what she's doing in the dark, she's groping her way downstairs. Not bothering to turn on a light. Her fingertips nearly able to feel the path just traced by Wina's fingers. Heat or something—though she can't quite sense it when she tries again, not even in her mind.

When she reaches the downstairs bedroom—of course—Wina is back in bed. As usual: asleep—yes—in Rose's old powder-blue bedroom. Myra smooths the covers over her mother-in-law's small bony frame hunched on the bed like a child—and *smelly. Phew! A bath today.* So hard to give lately, Wina resisting mightily, asking suspiciously, "Do you take baths?" Will incontinence be next?

And Wina is suddenly snoring like an ox! Louder than Frank's formidable snores. Shocking to hear such a hardy and ugly noise—and so loud!—issuing forth from such a tiny and weak-looking elderly woman. *Poor Wina*, Myra thinks, surprised by the force of her own compassion. Not long till the end, probably. Or a nursing home, if she and Frank can ever bring themselves to that. Or afford it! Especially these days!

Myra stands for a minute, bent over the bed where she read so many bedtime stories to Rose and simply lets the familiar noise wash over her. Not music, of course, but something else. Something human. It's pouring over and through her.

Then she's not hearing it anymore—not Wina at all but something more, faint but clear. She hears words in her ears, lets her own lips silently form those words: "This too shall pass." Wina's old motto, her personal key to the world: *Beowulf*. Exactly the notion that's needed. Yes, *Beowulf*, Edwina's response to every disaster, once. And there'd been so many disasters! Wina's father's sudden death coming first, when she was fourteen. Then the death of her first young husband, from TB.

And drinking—both Ed's Dad and Wina's sister Cora alcoholics. Then the unhappy marriages. And Wina *did* marry three times after all: "Marriage is just another word for trouble," as Wina once loved to joke. Plus the Depression, World War II, then Frank's Dad sent off to Korea though he was far too old—all that. Edwina teaching days, going to school at night for decades, to earn a teaching degree and get certification.

Too. Nearly what Myra herself did. Studying history as well as she could, here, working so damned hard for a decade or more to enter a field she loved—just to become a second-rater. A part-timer, "an adjunct." A mere shadow in the university world.

Like Edwina these days, Myra thinks. Then: *No. Much worse to be nearly a ghost: Alzheimer's.* The gradual loss of one's mind, one's *self*. A real curse, to end life losing your mind. Myra sinks into Edwina's old plaid rocker they shipped from Chicago, feeling breathless, thinking that she and Edwina *are* so much alike after all. Except, despite everything, her own life is far easier.

Out the window, there's the snow—falling into its own pure light, so peaceful and timeless. Bluish-white and luminous, even in the dark. Beautiful flakes, lacy and delicate—but so huge! Still so thick! When Myra stands for a better look, the backyard is brimming with snow. Snow up to the window frame, as high as the fence posts, snow just everywhere! No end yet to this damned blizzard! It has the look of—what was it?

A secret stay-at-home day. Wasn't that what Rose as a little girl called snow days—snowbound for a few hours or a whole magical day? School and work and every bit of ordinary life canceled. A holiday they always needed. A bit of peace.

Maybe needed now too, Myra's thinking. Just as much? But surely that's impossible. *Peace?* For herself and Edwina and Frank?

He certainly needs it most, of course, with all the cutbacks going on at the airport. Handing out pink slips day after day to friends. Maybe his own next. Her part-timer's job is only semester-to-semester too, not to mention the abysmal pay. And so many worries over Wina—how will they ever afford a nursing home?

And now Rose. Atop Wina's chest of drawers, she sees the neatly embroidered motto Rose gave to her Gram at Christmas, its flowery silken letters glowing under dark glass:

THE BEST AND MOST BEAUTIFUL THINGS IN THE WORLD CANNOT BE SEEN OR EVEN HEARD. THEY MUST BE FELT WITH THE HEART.
—HELEN KELLER

Myra recalls then, through Edwina's snores, all the Siberian women she's met in the last decade. Though why on earth have they come to mind now? Maybe last night's course? Siberians just everywhere in Alaska since glasnost and the fall of communism, women so like herself and Edwina—amazingly like—especially Alexandra, the friend she knows best, a dear soul, a historian from Magadan who's now hiding out in Moscow with her son, so that he—schizophrenic—won't be sent to a work camp, still in place in Russia under Putin. Alexandra working quietly as a private language tutor, as poorly paid as herself and then some—with not just her son but a sick older sister to care for.

And Myra recalls Alexandra's beloved historic tale of Veniaminov, later St. Innocent, sent from Irkutsk to Alaska in 1824 as an Orthodox missionary, an arduous trip. He was twenty-six, traveling with his widowed mother, his younger brother, his small son, and pregnant wife, who gave birth to their first surviving daughter on shipboard. Her fifth pregnancy; they'd already lost three infants at birth. An amazing man, he held Alaska's first coed bilingual schools, often traveling by kayak or dogsled to villages along the coast to transcribe Tlingit: its first written words his work, the effort that kept that language alive.

How Alexandra loves this tale! But a note from his journal is what Myra loves: how, after wintering in Sitka that first year, the family set off by small ship to his mission in Unalaska; July 1825, another difficult trip. And, he noted, when the exhausted group finally made shore "the first thing our women did was go off to pick berries." Berry season. Of course. They couldn't resist. Old skills transformed to suit Alaska, change as a way of life for resourceful women. Unreligious Myra smiles at this: women just like her Siberian friends.

"Wedded to change," as Alexandra sighed once, joking about the horrors of being set adrift in postcommunist Russia: "So difficult, Myra. Though we're much better off of course." But tossed alive into a new "freedom" that often felt like a curse: jobs gone, money devalued, work lost, lives transformed, everything tossed up into the air.

Maybe like driving in a blizzard? That loss of all boundaries. The sheer impossibility of any clarity of forward movement. Terrifying—but strangely exhilarating too—

"Now they'll join us." Karl's joke about the fall of communism in Russia, over a long-ago cup of coffee: "free but damned—in debt up to their eyeballs like proper capitalists."

How she loved him! Why didn't they act? Cowardice? Fear? But no: *decency*. Good sense. And Frank. How could they betray Frank? Karl liked Frank, and she of course was *married* to him—how could she and Karl make an ugly thing of such a beautiful one? She and Karl—and Frank too—were decent people, honorable people. People who cherish love. Like Rose.

Ah, love again. What is it? Anyway she still loves snow, doesn't she? Its beauty and mystery, that transformative power—just as Edwina does—or did once. And Rose.

Life is such a puzzle, Myra's thinking, *nothing like the fixed order of history, the recorded past*. Though in truth maybe equally paradoxical, like Veniaminov's family history: his beloved wife, Ekaterina, dying in Siberia in 1839, in Irkutsk, the hometown they'd longed to retire to for a quiet life after she bore five more children in Alaska, all now motherless. And he instead cast deeper into duty in the church. *All human lives tangled in mystery?*

But maybe that's what Edwina wanted to say upstairs in the dark? That the three of us *do* have so much in common: Edwina and Myra and Rose. *Maybe I should stop worrying about Rose? I must trust her*, Myra decides, *let her be herself and live her own life. If Rose loves somebody, he has to be decent, an honorable person. He must be a fine man.*

And surely *this* is the triangle that matters: *Wina, Myra, Rose.*

Myra sees it clearly: three strong, capable women, generous and loving, born for this world. Each of us a small part of some vast unknown schemata, some grand endeavor that can't be understood in advance. Edwina's chair seems to rock on its own while Myra considers that. The motion, even the padding of the old chair Rose loves too offering its badly needed solace. To be savored, Myra knows it. To be enjoyed and respected.

Like Wina's still so-human snores: back at full volume again. And French toast! That's what she'll make for breakfast—she's hungry for it. A Sunday breakfast: Edwina's recipe, laced with a capful of brandy—Frank's best-loved of any breakfast on earth. Everybody's favorite in this family. Today there'll be time.

Smallpox

(Notes from a sleep-deprived, overeager visiting writer, Lower Kuskokwim School District, Southwest Alaska)

"You have one!" shouts the squinting boy. He's leaping up to peer at Anna through the thick lenses of his glasses. They're toy-size glasses held on in back by elastic, while he bobs/bounces/points/jiggles/hops/blinks/sinks in place [like her mind here] sitting again. [5? 6?] He's cross-legged on the crowded floor, far right, second row: "A little hole. Here."

Each word//*again*//surges [*memory*//flare and burn of//*again*//here and//*again*] to cut [*clear-cut*/a forest?] through Anna's perpetual stage fright. She's *shy* as ever but so *wordy*: garrulous/stiff/fiery/cold, and self-conscious too: in classroom after classroom, for days. [Inching/inching towards *revelation*//self-immolation//: Self or {*mask*} then and which part?] And it's not English exactly but something else in his mouth: a Second Language [to swim in/underwater/under ice/duress/*Native Tongue*/it's not Yup'ik] while his thumb probes an invisible spot just above his left eyebrow: a *pock-?*

-mark. Yes. Anna is nodding//again//: yes [*acne*/years of], going on and on with this tale for first graders, for students of all ages [*self* as a voice then? *VOICE*: still/small?] in English: at Nightmute, Kwigillingok, Tuntutuliak, then at Mekoryuk on Nunivak Island.

Of snow out the window that lasts and lasts [stiff satin: *snow*]. Faded boardwalks like lines drawn through the village and fish drying on rickety wooden racks between the coast and the box-houses [not *igloos*: like sturdy shacks/tiny/huddled: on stilts]. Three-seater plane/her first: *bush plane*, and real *tundra:* flat, flat, flat. Japanese-car-size wood sledges pulled behind snow-machines through windchill to a school, from the airstrip and then back. Scarlet sunset on snow, and of how you might—anyone—[treeless/*sky*]—someday become—*yes*/if you try—a writer.

Because you love stories. And because you live in Alaska where there are so many. Stories everywhere, far too few of them ever written {*poured/pored*} onto paper [*far too—for?*]. And because you love hearing them over and over, told by people you love or maybe people you don't know at all. [Same as? No joke: *joke: truth*/frozen as *paradox?*] Because you want them to live beyond the—scrawny/thick-walled/gnarled imperfection of—WORDS. [And not words only but *self* too. Yet selfish even to try?]

And because the words play in your head like music—pictures or their tales/tails, like this *WIND*—or like the wandering moose: three together/so rare—*trudging*: on foot//FOOT//cloven hooves—through the backyard snowdrifts [at home: thirty years of /*suburban/*: *White Alaska*] in Fairbanks: trees//*TREES*//snowy woods of this pale//*light*//thin snake of highway [not board-] like a message for Alaskan children: *snowdrifts.*

Words like songs or like stories, dances, like sculpture or carving, bead-work. Parkies and fur hats: *on.* And the tiny hand-stitched doll-size gut raincoat hanging high//Yup'ik: a signboard: word*less*//in the school hallway//*display*//*-play*//life the art then? Words no measure of—*ever?* (*LOVE*//as//*hours?*)

Words like snowdrifts sculpted beyond this window. Strings of geese in the spring and again in fall honking the skies of our minds//*ours*//always and never, forever.

[Like Siberia? Not hers—five years in her mind/heart and its gifts: trinkets? A few days only/weeks/a tourist/and/suburban//*again*//self-deluding? Souvenirs only, spread out/here/on the table: *LOVE*/Siberia?]

And of how Grandma would ride for hours across the map of St. Louis on streetcars and buses on Sundays after church to bring stories to Anna: "Exactly your age then." How Grandma—[exactly Anna's own/*age?* 55? But so—{*old*}. Older than, then? In 1946. Like the just-fired teacher/third grade/plump, sweet-faced, so kind looking, from Boston/thirty years of//*here*//and how could they?] How Grandma {petite, sweet-faced—*too*: like the teacher—and Anna herself?} would stop at the transfer point, step into Koob's Bakery minutes before it closed, then walk boldly up to the tall, strong, mean-faced, snippy young woman behind the glass counter—wanting to close up//*again*//.

Grandma: bent-fingered/in Enna Jetticks-like/but a copy/shoes//*FOOT*// for work, and the dark blue flower-sprigged dress with its delicate lace collar and matching straw hat, navy blue [from South Broadway/the sidewalk sale] with cherries among dark leaves on its brim. Everything "God's good gift," from strudel or a sunny day to an automobile wreck where nobody died. Dark brooch at her damp neck//*DARK*//and the pearls—bouncing across [Evening in Paris] her chest: pop pearls, pale blue, from Famous-Barr where she'd had to lie [her age], a widow already outlasting her children, to get work. Selling towels, sheets, dishes sometimes—a saleslady.

Until they discovered her true age. [But how? And why? Who?] And what age? Surely older? And she loved it—didn't she? Self-supporting [*self*] and busy. Best time of her—*TIME*. {*Babushka*, a grandmother.} Too. Eons from//again and again//Alaska, Siberia, Paris//*true age*//eons—anyone?

"I brought this bakery trash, I couldn't resist." Sound of voice/dialogue/poetry in it [first money-job/last/55—or older?] bending to kiss Anna's cheek/forehead/squeezing of fingers. Smells of stale tea, dentures, Ivory soap, ferment of bosom: Paris. And foot powder/Blue Cross/in her handbag. While Grandma placed the white-paper package with its white-paper tape on the kitchen table: *bakery trash*. [But what? Anna can't just now—robbery/sudden—recall a bite/no/never/not ever/tasting/a bite of it, no, and why not?]

Apricot strudel, maybe that? Seven favorite: bakery—[Two words or one?] "Choose any . . ." [*Choose!* Promiscuous then because she loves all? But how could you—anyone/ever/choose only] ". . . seven!" [Woman/writer/slut/whore because you love—? But men do too: *WORDS*. And yes—*men*: like Grandma: not a joke.]

How Anna would pat the couch beside her for Grandma [". . . exactly your age," Anna says it again: *echo/againanda*] and then she'd request it (again): "Tell about when you were sick."

"Oh, that one again—you always love that one, don't you?"

How—while Anna hunted the fragrant sticks of—vagrant/lost/hidden, disappeared and crinkly in the silvery paper—*gum*—deep in the dark/many/pockets of the fat black handbag till found and tamed—chewed—

{"*askimowew*: Cree: he eats it raw": Merriam-Webster's}

//chew/*zhevat*: Russian: "*Mad*" because they talk and//*TALK*//endless tales??//

<*winter stories*: Athabascan, end: "*And now we have eaten a bit of The Winter.*">

WINTER . . . snow . . . for weeks . . . a week . . . seven itself: months of winter. And seven as magic in stories/because/*TIME?* Lives falling as/leaves//flakes//skin?

How Grandma peeled it away. *SKIN*//her skin. *All.* How, with the fever gone, she had to peel it away. But before that so sick, sick for weeks—forever it seemed—and in bed. Not able to eat. Asleep ["*Sleep*/perchance to . . ."] while so many died or got sicker, but not she: a story.

Peeling it as she must, her skin, as her mother told her she must, carefully placing the peeled and shriveled bits in a clean glass jar. Putting on the lid, twisting it down, standing up from the bed carefully [in little-girl hand-me-down/youngest of four/nightgown] and then—wobbly and weak still—digging a hole by the back steps with her mother to bury the jar so nobody else would catch it: *smallpox.*

"And then Grandma was well." (A story. Seven times or fifteen?)

"Because in those days they had no medicine. Eighteen hundred ninety-five/one hundred years ago: *smallpox.*" Anna says it once more to taste/caress//*WORDS*//Mother Tongue: tenth time or sixteenth (. . . *seven favorite/Your assignment for the rest of your//I expect an A+//life: choose [lose] seven/any language/change them whenever you/for the rest of your/Mother/any/Tongue: FOOT. Two feet to stand on if you speak two/or even more. Someday, some people: to write, think, translate, remember/Yup'ik and then Cup'ik/languages . . .*) and *pox/pock*: a little hole, yes, like/a/*pocket.* But:

"You have one!"

$\approx$

Sleeping on the floor/*again*/the last night/library floor/as the first night/gym mat, folded, Anna hears it again, *echo: You have one!*

She gets up and frowns, thinking/thinking (again): first of this place [magical—but *real:* home: *Alaska*: {*kolyaska*: a word in Russian: a carriage/

dark/and frozen/in winter/a journey then?} one life as—*DARK*] new snow again/seven/*WIND*, and—yes, of her own life: five wiggly and hopping grandsons, nearly babies. *To love that much/easy {joy} what you live//for//*—

But. To *escape* family too, always//*LIFE*//to search: *a search*//because, no, Grandma had none. No *pock*. No, never a one. Except for that long/ huge, flat, roundish/oval/Paris-in/and much more than a *pock*/on her left/ *scar*/upper arm—her vaccination—

And, in the red-spined many-volumed children's encyclopedia/wonderful, each bit its own small/jewel of a/story: *Smallpox*/virus/cowpox/18th century/universal vaccination by Edw. Jenner, English physician, 1796. One hundred ninety-nine—nearly two hundred years—

S also: *Scarlet.* *-fever (scarlatina)* caused by strep// . . . *penicillin*//treatment but no real//*of course*//cure . . . /rash and fever/days or weeks//skin peeling away—

Of course.

Alaska: Russian contact//smallpox//many deaths/epidemic: Yukon-Kuskokwim delta: beyond the reach of vaccine, 1838: HERE.

//*Skin*//those small bright faces looking up, trusting and rapt, her own face hot in the dark: *smallpox.* Over and over: and how could she? Thirty years in Alaska—and how could she—how could she not *think*? Shame of: *scarlet//error//not* "LOVE."

To children. Apologize?

But how? Impossible. A failure//*again*?

But. Love *is.* So much/easy-as-difficult. More always than the words// *WORDS*//.

CHOOSE: lose: jobs/lost, children/buried, loves/drifting away—

Never disease anyway, love. Always gift/accident/shock/no choice.

And, yes: You have one!

Scarlet fever/two words again/far more than. Though the words are. Always and always. Yes: she's been given: *againanda*—

Anna-in-love again//*no choice*//end as beginning. Wind/rattling the/ metal, heavy/front/school doors in the dark: *Always/always/so much more/ than she gave.*

Air

Where to begin? It's not August but May, and Aunt Louie is pushing the binoculars up against her glasses and peering through the windshield. "It's a Toro, Rosie," she's saying. I know then that she isn't focusing on another sandhill crane, like the long-necked thin wedge of bird she pointed out as we turned off Farmers Loop, its gawky form rising into the air above the marsh, where we're headed, with its spindly legs still dangling.

"A Toro?" I wonder if she's renaming Mt. McKinley. It's visible tonight—*Denali*, the Great One as the Athabascans call it, like a vast snowy pyramid one hundred fifty miles south of Fairbanks. I can imagine Louie seizing on the ghostly mountain as a bull—in rut probably. But her binoculars are pointing east, toward the parking lot of the only building around, a cinderblock mass off to our left, a bikers' bar called the Grubstake.

"Yes," she says, "a Toro." And she plumps the binoculars down on the seat between us with a satisfied grunt. I'm bent over the steering wheel of the minivan trying to see across her when I figure it all out—when I see the snowblower perched on the roof of the bar in a shallow valley created by the confluence of two low angles. It's huge, a handheld snowblower like the one my Aunt Louie—Louise Burns is her full name—had spread out across the floor of her cabin when I picked her up. Louie was crouched in the parlor among the greasy-looking metal parts, trying to rebuild the thing into a rototiller. That one is—or was—a Toro too, and it's the same faded orange-red color.

"How do you suppose they got it up there?" she asks—and not out of idle curiosity, I'm certain. Her cabin sits at what Ted, my husband, calls "the tail-hole end" of Solstice Lane, and its turreted roof also has glaciering and condensation problems—I mean that it leaks. Heating the place sends hot air out of various turrets and windows and angles, forming ice sheets above and below the logs and tarpaper, batting and shingles to thaw and refreeze all winter, on and off, seven months of the year. Exactly what the roof of this rundown-looking bar must do, I'm guessing—a condition complicated last winter by the heavy snowfall we had. Ted jokes—sometimes even to Louie herself—that her solution is to burn the cabin down: "clean it and burn it." Though Louie's been told by the agricultural extension guy to try simplifying the angles of the roof. An approach Louie sees as a desecration nearly as bad as burning.

Instead, she shovels away each successive snowfall just as these Grubstake people must do, though in her case by hand. All this shoveling was how she got tennis elbow, started acupuncture, then developed what she calls "my engagement with air." Which is why she bought the binoculars that are leaning against my thigh—to enjoy the view from her roof. One of Louie's numerous mottos is *What you can't change, enjoy!*

Actually, the go-round with acupuncture was brief. But it led to Eastern religion, a fascination that promises to be, well—God knows what. Lengthy maybe. And probably linked up in Louie's mind with her most enduring new interest: *Air.*

"A block and tackle? A pulley?" That's what I say, though what I imagine is four or five of the hefty Hell's Angels types I associate with the Grubstake straining their bellies against those leather jackets they wear, hoisting it up there.

"No," she says, exhaling the words, "*person* power." By now we're close to the point below the highway where the old road dead ends, at the small marsh my aunt has mapped out for us—or my ex-aunt, I suppose, since Louie's been divorced from Uncle Martin for several years. But I didn't divorce Louie, and even IRS forms have special names and categories for near relatives and such, both former and future. Have you noticed that? It's true. Anyway, we've passed the place. We're a quarter mile or so beyond the bar, deep into a wilderness of stunted black spruce and marsh. But when I turn off the ignition and open the driver's door, I still hear the faint thump and twang of country-rock music billowing forth on the breeze from the Grubstake.

Louie leans out the passenger door to pull on the waders I've brought. They're the usual long, stiff, tan-colored things in a pants-like configuration. I borrowed them from Ted's stepdad, my father-in-law, Ward Embert, a semi-retired lawyer who tonight as always prefaced his remarks about Louie with a puzzled frown then his usual words: "*Oh, you mean that hippie woman Martin was involved with?*" Though Louie and Uncle Martin were married something like twenty-seven years and Louie is too young by a decade or more to be considered a true hippie.

Ward enjoys dipnetting for salmon—his use for the waders. But Louie has come for cattails. She saw them from the highway this afternoon and convinced me that when I'd put the kids to bed, we should go out and cut some. "Plenty for the both of us, Rosie," those were her words.

"Rosalind, just look," she's calling out now. Though I despise that name, as she very well knows. She's lifting her face, beaming, while her glasses glint at me in the sunlight.

It's way past ten p.m. and still light—that glorious, pearly slanted springtime light that, in the first weeks after seven long months of winter, *does* make you feel like you've taken up residence in heaven. So I grin back, watching while her fingers smooth the rubber of the waders upward—a hopeless task since they're much too big.

"Isn't it amazing how they've managed to survive the winter?" says Louie.

I have to admit that the cattails are beauties, tall and perfect, as thick-bodied as corn dogs. Nevertheless, I'm wondering what will happen when we touch them. They'll probably go up like dandelion fluff, I'm thinking, vanishing into thin air. Though I myself do not intend to wade off into that yucky-looking marsh to test out my hypothesis.

Anyway, we only have the one pair of waders, and my aunt is standing up in them taking tentative tiny stomping steps back and forth while she slides her arms through the shoulder straps, with the things bunching around her ankles like a pair of oversized tights that Tanya, my youngest daughter, likes to borrow from Rissie, the oldest one. Louie's adjusting the straps in that fussy way of hers—which won't really take up all that length—when I see the wasps.

"*Duck, Louie!*" I shout, and she does, so that the first wasp and then several others deflect off the left shoulder strap of the waders rather than hitting her neck. I'll later decide what's happened is that we've driven up onto the nests of some burrowing wasps by the marsh. Because I've read up on wasps and hornets and yellow jackets and such since then, trying to figure it all out. Aunt Louie's my best friend, I suppose, though most of the things we do together turn into minor disasters. This time it won't be cattails or air or snow on the roof after all, I'm thinking—it'll be wasps, though the only insect we've come prepared for is mosquitoes. Anywhere you go in Alaska, except when there's snow, you must be ready for mosquitoes. Though with Louie, you never know whether just one disaster will be it. Wasps may be only the start, I decide, as I grab my purse and begin to swing it at them. Tonight I'd've predicted mandala symbolism.

Mandala symbolism is why we signed up for the enhanced computer course at the downtown center in the first place. Which ended that Wednesday afternoon in May, causing us to be out on the highway earlier, coming home. Louie has a theory that use of computers—or computer art forms, as she calls this stuff—ties into "universal consciousness," whatever that is, by tapping the mandala. Because computers extend human minds, and we can't escape the simple fact, Louie says, that human minds, created by nature and extended out logically, only create—well, more *Nature* I guess. Capital N. She saw her first natural representation of the form—or animate maybe, live, in motion—an example of the mandala, I mean—while she shoveled her roof last fall.

Ravens, clustering in the air. That's what it was rather than an actual mandala. Which I think of as static, of course. Still. To this day I see the mandala as static.

The next one was an aurora, Northern Lights, a week or so after the ravens, sending her off to punch at her keyboard for several days—which I can hardly imagine—the aurora borealis looking like a mandala, I mean. Though I know that Louie, despite many other significant flaws and faults, does not lie. Hardly ever.

"DUCK, LOUIE," I shout again, louder. And she does. Or more like dives. Back into the passenger seat of the minivan while I throw it into reverse and floor the accelerator and back out of there fast as possible, both of us forgetting entirely about the cattails. Anyway, to make a long story shorter, all this was May as I've said, and we're well into August now, Louie and I in picture hats—hers beige, mine pale green—standing out in the yard next to her cabin like princesses in a fairy tale while Ted takes photos of us as the last step of—yes, you've guessed it—Louie's wedding. She was stung only a few times, but that made us race into the Grubstake, where she met Lance.

He's a Texan. A veteran of the first Gulf War who was tending bar at the Grubstake—still does, in fact, though he's now anti-war—and Louie got to know him when he came to her cabin later, to help her reassemble her Toro. After the only slightly inebriated men from the bar—I know you've guessed all this—hauled theirs down from the roof to show her. Once they'd tended to her stings. With beer. Dab it on cold, a little bit'll do, they said—true, apparently.

Lance is fourteen years younger than Louie and not all that good-looking. But then neither of them seems to care much about looks. Louie says fourteen is one of her sacred numbers, and Lance gets as high on numerology as he does on beer—or mandalas or log cabins or engine overhauls or whatever. Like getting himself a Harley distributorship in Siberia, in Yakutsk, our Sister City in Fairbanks, his latest scheme, which Lance swears will make him and Louie filthy rich. He's that kind of person too, always up or down about something, just like Louie—including gardening. As an example, since May they've not only rebuilt the Toro but turned most of Louie's yard over to potatoes and carrots and gorgeous heads of red-leaf lettuce, which you can't really see in these photos.

None of which truly proves that Lance is a wholesome individual. As I've tried and tried again and again to tell Louie. But then when has Aunt Louie ever listened to me? Or to anybody, for that matter.

But anyhow, as luck would have it, Louie isn't really allergic to wasps as we first feared when the stings began to swell up and turn grotesque and red like they did, right after she was stung. So that we *did* have to stop at the Grubstake—it was a medical necessity, not just fate or something. Had she been truly allergic, which is what Lance for one told her immediately, she'd already've been dead *then*—a couple of people have already died this summer of stings. Which I nevertheless do believe influenced Louie to suspect, as she so often does, that every event thereafter—such as Lance and their relationship—was part of a rebirth experience. All of which led—of course—directly to this outdoor wedding. Sheer logic, as Ted likes to say.

And it's a good thing she *isn't* allergic. Because I haven't even had time to signal to Ted and the girls, or to Lance—or to any of the guests there in the yard, including the Hell's Angels who've staked out the farthest edges of the little crowd, near the woods, maybe hoping to protect the kegs of beer. It's after the guitar player, Vladimir, who's a Russian and a part-time geology student who also teaches part-time at the university, has stopped playing—and the justice of the peace for a day, Louie's neighbor Enna, has just finished up the ceremony—but anyway, there's been absolutely no chance to signal to the crowd to cover their heads—as I would've liked to do, and as I certainly should have. Because the biggest swarm of wasps I've ever in my life glimpsed is descending from nowhere heading right for Louie—and for me, for that matter. Because there I stand like a fool next to her as matron of honor, captured for all time in this photo I've got in my hand.

Though not one wasp shows up in the photo. Just the two of us ducking like idiots while they fly right over our heads, above our hats, invisible to Kodak. This is the kind of thing Louie does to me—always, again and again, honestly.

Anyway, just looking at the photo, I remember everything so clearly it feels like I'm shouting it all over again: *DUCK, LOUIE!* And we're in the process of ducking—we honestly are—like Louie I do not lie, a fact that tends to be strengthened, believe me, by an experience such as this one—when I see, suddenly, the thing I'm trying to tell.

That the swarm of wasps flying over our heads—which are paper wasps this time, I assume, from a wasp colony nearby with one of those huge, bulbous paper nests hanging in the air like a Chinese lantern. That's how I picture it anyway, off in the woods beyond the yard, lit by a shaft of afternoon sunlight. Luminous and beautiful. Though what I've read online about wasps doesn't really explain any of this stuff at all.

But, let the facts speak for themselves, as Ted always tells me. These wasps have made—honest to God, though the photos show not one wasp, not a bit of it—*are* making in fact, as Ted snaps this very photo—an actual mandala shape. It hung there for twenty seconds or so, nearly still, hovering above us. Like a swarm of wedding guests kneading the air, I swear it.

Power Play

"Impossible to describe what it's like to live in this place," I say. The temperature sign at the police department reads minus thirty-six degrees. We're driving through skimpy ice fog, ghostly gray wisps of the stuff that hang in the air like tatters of torn gauze. Maybe ice fog is a sickly cousin to the Northern Lights somehow fallen to earth? If so, are we *in* the aurora? I think that too but don't say it. One rare phenomenon can't explain another I decide, while I grip the steering wheel and ponder a bumper sticker on the truck ahead of us, a phantasm in plumes of fog: *EAT MOOSE ~ 12,000 WOLVES CAN'T BE WRONG!!!*

It's midafternoon, January 2012, not much traffic, and the streets of downtown Fairbanks are strung with Christmas lights. "Wha'd'ya mean?" asks my great-aunt Patsy from the passenger seat. "It's cold. Dark. What's to describe?" Huge crocheted-looking electric snowflakes hang frost-covered and motionless in a long row stretching down Cushman Street. They're creamy white, luminous, and red taillights of a few cars and one commercial van dim then sharpen, poking through bluish plumes of fog and exhaust.

"I'm asking what you mean, Charlotte," Aunt Patsy repeats, a bit louder. "*Very* cold. *Very* dark." The truck's other sticker reads *ALASKAN GRANDMAS KICK BOOTIE.*

"Got that right." Nelda speaks up distinctly from the back seat where she sits among sacks stuffed with groceries, her plump dark face glowing in the

Toyota's rearview mirror from a spot squeezed between her own goodies in black cloth sacks and mine and Aunt Patsy's in the store's frozen-stiff white plastic. Does Nelda mean Aunt Patsy got it right, I wonder, or can she mean me, just thinking aloud? Maybe she means both of us?

When I raise my foot from the brake pedal, the tires of the Toyota bounce slightly: ice patches left by the snowplow rather than the usual freezing and going square after an hour in the parking lot at Bentley Mall Safeway while we shopped. I lift my heavy boot more carefully and we inch ahead, *clunk-clunk-clunk*, turning right while the stoplight on Tenth holds green. "Just—*impossible*," I repeat. The afternoon fog has an absurd power that's making the stoplights look decorative, or maybe drunken. They're manic and glittery, intensely bright and clear. Could the foul air be playing with my mind?

"What *do* you mean?" asks Aunt Patsy for a third time. "It's just January like always, Charlotte. Durned cold. Cold as heck."

"Not that," I say. "The distance, the isolation, the beauty. This toxic winter air. The utter strangeness and—*uniqueness*. Our way of life. The absolute freedom too. How you're bounced between desolation and exhilaration. Why we stay."

"Every place is unique," Aunt Patsy answers like a sigh. "Where d'ya park around here?" She points at Sadler's Furniture lot that I still think of as J.C. Penney's, mostly from childhood visits: Penney's moved out decades ago. "I'll wait in the car if it's a long hike," she says while I maneuver towards the site. My great-aunt is tiny, gnarled-looking, like a gnome carved from wood perched beside me as I peer across her at traffic. She's ninety-one and the reason I came to Alaska for a visit nearly thirty years ago, then stayed.

This is the year of the Farthest North Occupy Wall Street, going on and on heroically in tiny Veteran's Plaza across from Sadler's, a feat nobody but me seems to appreciate. Not one person I know sees the occupation for the wonder it is, with its frost-covered wall tent rising from deep snow next to the gazebo where people hold picnics and play music in summer. The tent's coming into view through the windshield, first its stovepipe then the frosty gray peak. *Amazing*, I think again. Something I want Aunt Patsy to see. And Nelda. "No way," I answer. "I'm not leaving you in a cold car. And some places *are*—well, just more unique than others, aren't they? Admit it."

"True enough, Choo," says Nelda, as if she's the self-appointed sanity judge for the day. "I'll stay with Patsy if you get out. Maybe you can leave the engine running."

Funny to be called *Choo* by somebody who's not family. "Right-oh," I say. Then: "Choo's a nickname Anthony gave me, Nelda. Did you know that? Years ago when our youngest was two and obsessed with Thomas the Tank Engine. I'd sit on the floor to play trains and the name stuck." Through Todd's *eleventh* birthday last week, I think with a bit of a pang. Nelda's laughing. She's probably heard the name from my husband, but not its origin. Nelda's been one of Aunt Patsy's caregivers for three months, and I like her.

"There 'tis," says Nelda, pointing toward the barely visible tent. "See it, Patsy?"

"Can you see from down there?" I ask Aunt Patsy, who remains silent, sunken into the front seat as she is. I'm pretty sure she hasn't seen the Occupy site before, though she lives only a few blocks away in a condo development full of seniors. She moved in three summers ago, after selling her beloved log house, and she rarely goes out anymore. Usually only when I drive her someplace, or if she calls a cab to take her to the liquor store, a thought that puts me back into worry mode quicker than the air is messing with my head: *I like giving business to the cabdrivers*, Aunt Patsy always says. *They have families to support and they're nice fellows.* I tried for ages not to criticize this plan, which she probably doesn't even do anymore. Not since Nelda and the two other caregivers came onto the scene, thanks to Aunt Patsy falling in her condo and the elder-alarm company getting involved.

I can see little puffs of Aunt Patsy's breath, though she doesn't answer. She's silent, eyes half-closed, frowning while the car churns ahead in the fog like my brain: *They've put the brakes on me*, Aunt Patsy also says, about the alarm company. I'm recalling that.

Well, she *is* ninety-one after all, and she *did* sensibly give up driving two years ago. Those were my thoughts even last year, why I didn't step in: me trying to prolong as long as possible what I see as my aunt's freedom. Her autonomy, her personal power. And she *did* choose to sign up for the elder alarm, suggested by her friends, so there's not much I can do. Anyway, Anthony says I tend to be a worrywart, so I'm trying to step back.

But Aunt Patsy insists on wearing the too-light, plaid-lined rust-colored jacket she has on, despite Nelda's complaints, and mine. And those checkered worn-out slip-on canvas shoes that she says give her balance, all of which worries me plenty. Plus old jeans and a jaunty-looking cane with a dog's head, and that small felt hat with the red feather that's disappearing in another puff of breath, which might be good enough—*warm* enough— for fall or summer. It looks like an alpine cap or a man's, like all the lightweight mannish stuff she usually wears, even at forty below. And *has* worn for decades, maybe always.

Aunt Patsy is a lesbian, something I didn't figure out till I was in my twenties, but that fact seems part of an ancient past. She's a retired pilot too—one of the first female pilots in the country, or the world—so she should know better, about both drinking and warm clothes. Her coat is the main reason I drop everything, if possible, and drive her out for groceries, or even liquor, mostly Alaskan beer and big bottles of Irish crème or Kahlua, whenever she asks, if I can. There's a bottle of Kahlua in one of the white sacks in the back seat, as a point of fact. She has an old parka and boots, of course, but she says they weigh her down. She hates the long black down coat I got her for Christmas: *I feel like a penguin*, she says. Today I've wrapped her up in it in the car, like a quilt.

"We'll just drive past a couple of times," I say. "We don't need to stop." The Toyota has a good heater, though it's slow to get up to full speed, and it's pumping mightily. I'm beginning to feel thawed out, almost cozy. "Are you warm enough?" I ask Aunt Patsy, and she nods. She's indulging me, I can tell.

"Comfy back here," says Nelda, though I see a puff of breath in the rearview mirror turning her brown face chalky. We'll drive Nelda home to South Fairbanks next, then I'll stay with Aunt Patsy till Nelda's relief lady—I think it's Tanya, a young Russian woman from Delta Junction—arrives. Nelda's old Impala broke down so she's pinched for rides.

Wall-to-wall caregivers like this cost a lot: *one arm and two legs*, says Aunt Patsy. But they're written into the elder-alarm contract, taking effect if the client falls or is hospitalized. Which Aunt Patsy was, hospitalized for ten days in October, though she insists she's OK: *They found nothing wrong*, she says repeatedly. Her doctor did take me aside and ask me to try to watch her drinking, try to help her cut back. But as I told him, she lives alone and she's always liked to drink. "Maybe she doesn't eat enough anymore," he said, and I promised to try. My New Year's resolution: bringing her nicely packaged, frozen but tempting homemade TV dinners culled from my family's meals, to microwave, plus lots of fresh fruit. Breathing this air can substitute for liquor, I suspect.

The Occupy people's army-surplus wall tent is planted like a square igloo across from city hall, which we're passing. It's a structure from the late nineteenth century like you might find anywhere but covered in hoarfrost and colored lights that twinkle in the midday dusk: "So pretty," Nelda's saying, not of the tent but the cheery city hall lights.

"Did you know it's the former Main School, Fairbanks' first public school, Old Main?" I ask Nelda. "People we know were part of its various incarnations: last elementary class, first junior high, last school district office, till its current use as city hall," I say, while Nelda nods. Then I tell how the Occupiers started out picketing at the library, even through Christmas—all day, ten or twenty people a day, till I feel like a tour guide: "Not so amazing maybe," I add, "except for the arctic gear: bunny boots and such. And the cold." I joined in one warm Saturday in October, but not once since. I'm ashamed to tell that.

You've got a lot on your plate, Anthony says loyally. I work mornings at Starbucks, take classes for a teaching degree, and I'm trying to write. Plus our three boys, and Aunt Patsy. It tears me up sometimes, being so busy: I love every bit till I start to feel, just once in a while, like an unpaid caregiver assisting Nelda. "The tent's spot here near city hall must be an attempt at visibility," I say aloud.

No Wall Street here, I'm thinking. But Veteran's Plaza is run by the borough, like all local parks, though the tent stirred up controversy at both Borough Assembly and City Council meetings. Last week the assembly took away the protestors' porta-potty. Which irate locals had demanded. The Occupiers now cross Cushman Street to use the restroom at the Presbyterian church, joining the homeless teens who sleep in a shelter at the church.

God, I think again for the umpteenth time: *All this in America! In Alaska!*

So far nobody has evicted the five or six remaining protestors I saw limping around at noon, stomping the fresh snow outside the tent when I drove to Aunt Patsy's. Smoke wafts from an angled stovepipe at the top of the tent, and a tall, long-haired young guy emerges through the tent flap as the Toyota clunks onward. I'm hoping Aunt Patsy can see the tent, and the guy, from her low-down spot in the passenger seat. He's dressed in layer upon dirty-looking layer, layers that nonetheless allow all that hair to flow—maybe he has dreadlocks; I can't be sure at this distance. Bushy hair pours out from a wool cap. Nobody else is around far as I can see, or maybe a woman, getting out of a car at the curb below the small hill at the site, carrying what looks like a potluck casserole.

"Look at all those signs," says Nelda. Protest signs are stacked around the curved edges of the gazebo in deep snow, so frost-covered you can read only a few from the car:

HIGHER TAXES FOR THE 1%

ONE FOURTH OF AMERICA'S CHILDREN LIVE IN POVERTY

POWER TO THE PEOPLE!!!

INCOME DISPARITY IS A NATIONAL CRIME

STOP LOW-WAGE SLAVERY!!

Those are the ones I see.

Increasing income disparity is something my great-aunt can't believe: *How can it be some new part of modern life?* That's what Aunt Patsy asks. We've discussed it. "When have the rich *not* been rich?" she says now, sighing, poking a mitten at her alpine hat.

"Richer. *Far* richer," I answer as always. Maybe a protest at minus thirty-six degrees won't change her mind but I have to try. Aunt Patsy is a lifelong liberal; her social and political views helped me form mine, and I want her to see the Occupiers with her own old eyes.

Nelda's views on the subject are unknown to me, but she speaks up again from the back seat: "That boy looks mighty sleepy, Choo. Do they sleep in that little tent?"

"Um-hum," I answer. "I think they've had the tent for a week or two."

"I read about it in the paper," Nelda says, though our local newspaper has devoted zero space to the protest. And not one photo, though they cover all the complaints at public meetings. "But I cain't see what those boys want people to *do*."

"Maybe just think about the problem," I say. "Wake us up. Maybe start a conversation about national values and lift our consciousness. I believe they take turns, Nelda. Shifts, so two or three sleep there. If the tent's empty, they'll be booted out."

"You have to work from *inside* the system," says Aunt Patsy in her cracked-sounding voice while another young guy emerges from the tent. The woman with the casserole, or what I think is a casserole, a big lump wrapped in bath towels, talks to the wild-haired one, passing the lump from her normal-sized gloved hands into his huge army-surplus mitted ones. The other guy approaches, stomping his feet for warmth. "They need to get jobs. Go to school to learn a useful trade, find a decent occupation. Make themselves part of the solution," says Aunt Patsy, speaking louder than I've heard her speak in ages.

"It takes money to go to school," I say. "Tuition's high. Not many jobs in winter. And you sound like a capitalist, Aunt Pat." She hates capitalists. And Republicans, *and* being called Pat. "I admire their gumption. I really do," I say. We're nearly past. I'm heading for Sadler's to turn and drive back up the street the other way for a second look.

"But don't you think it's a bit of a game for those white boys, Choo?" asks Nelda. "Being poor, I mean? Aren't they playing a bit at being poor?"

"A cold game, if so," I say, beginning a too-wide U-turn in Sadler's lot a bit too fast. I'm hoping I won't lose my temper, which is short lately, and I'm trying hard not to.

"My Richard had one devil of a time finding work last year," Nelda goes on, speaking of her son. I know she lives with Richard and his family, in a mother-in-law apartment above their garage. "But he got on as a watchman at the mall. Doin' OK now."

So Richard's a rent-a-cop! I think, but I say: "Today reminds me of power outages in the old days, Nelda." Maybe I'm trying to avert my anger by changing topics while we gawk. Defuse what I'm definitely feeling: My face is hot, and my lips feel tight. "In 1992 Vincent, our oldest boy, was barely a toddler when we had that September snowstorm that broke so many trees and power lines," I'm saying. "Remember that?"

"Oh yes," says Nelda, while Aunt Patsy mutters something I can't hear. "My first year. First winter in Alaska."

"Power was out for days, remember? I'd wrap Vincent up in stacks of blankets. Try to keep him in an armchair to stay warm. Impossible. He'd crawl out of his bindings. We kept the pipes in the house from freezing with the propane oven and a fireplace. It was—fun, I guess. Like a game. Why did you come to Alaska, Nelda?"

"My dad helped build the Alaska Highway, the Al-Can. Through Canada during the Second War," she says. "That was 1942 and '43, before he met Momma. He was in the Yukon in a service regiment. Which was what black folks were put into in those days, Choo. The military didn't trust ordinary black men to fight. That was the way of things till Korea, when they finally desegregated the military. Maybe you didn't know all that?"

"Well, I did and I didn't," I say. "You explain it well, Nelda. It's a bit like Aunt Patsy being a WASP, I guess." I see Nelda nodding in the rearview mirror, and Aunt Patsy looks as if she's nodding off while I maneuver in the parking lot, ending my U-turn and cooling down some. "Same principle, I mean. Women's Air Service Pilots, the WASPs, were the first U.S. female pilots, but they weren't officially recognized. They weren't even considered a part of the military back then; they were not appreciated. Right, Aunt Patsy?" She's silent. "They flew military planes. Important work ferrying badly needed planes across the nation," I say, "but they weren't treated fairly."

"Yes," says Nelda. "Same kinda thing. Dad didn't want to come back up North. Too many mosquitoes, too much mud." Nelda's laughing, bouncing among the grocery sacks while I head toward the street for another look at the Occupiers. "But the North caught my imagination," she says. "Burt, my hubby, wasn't interested either, but when Richard went into the army, don't you know they sent him North!" Nelda chuckles. "He must be like his momma. Wanted to stay on when his tour ended, and Rosemary liked Alaska too. When Burt passed away, I came up for a visit and stayed. For the freedom, like you said, Choo. And as an adventure. Wanted to be near my grandkids too."

I'm nodding. "Aren't family ties amazingly powerful? So your dad helped build the Al-Can, Nelda? That's interesting. Quite a feat. Beautiful country, but so empty. Rugged too. Anthony and I nearly went nuts driving it with our boys. Three times down and up."

Aunt Patsy stirs in her seat. She rarely talks about being a WASP anymore, or about teaching flying, then working for decades as a ticket agent for a local airline. "Charlotte's boys are a handful," she says, turning her head a bit towards Nelda, speaking as if she's trying to rouse herself from slumber. "But we love 'em." I'm back in the traffic lane, ready to enter the street, then I enter it. No traffic to speak of.

"Amazing how we all ended up here," I say.

"My great-grandmomma was a slave," says Nelda suddenly, speaking softly, dreamily. As if musing about the past is stirring something deep inside. "In Louisiana."

"*Really*," I say. A pathetic response, but I say it. "Did you know her?"

"She truly *was* a slave," Nelda answers. "Not a game. She died the year before I came along, Choo, 1946. I did see photos. She was so *tiny*. Just like Patsy. My momma says she used to say what kept her alive through slavery was Lincoln. Can you feature *that*?" Nelda's laughing. "Thinking about that skinny, serious-looking white man with the big tall hat who *cared*, who understood people like her, Momma told me. And of course later on her own children too. They kept her alive and hopeful. *Hoping and hopping*, she'd say, according to Momma. Lived to be one hundred and three. For their sakes."

I pull the Toyota into a parking spot behind the casserole woman's Chevrolet, though I'm not sure why. It feels like my eyes are tearing up. I reach back and squeeze Nelda's purple-mittened hands. Something in me wants to acknowledge the spooky feeling in the car. That power. Not from Nelda exactly, who squeezes my big-gloved hands right back, but from her story. "What an amazing woman, Nelda," I say. Then, absurdly: "I've got an extra gallon of milk." I say it too loudly, mostly to Nelda. "I'm giving it to those boys."

"Wait," says Nelda. She rummages in her handbag while I climb out of the driver's seat and take a bag from the back seat that holds one plastic gallon bottle of two-percent milk. Nelda pulls a crisp, new-looking ten-dollar bill from her handbag and pushes it at me. "Give 'em this too, Choo," she says, while steam billows from the car.

"Oh Nelda, that's—so generous of you," I say. Then I do it, walk right up to the stomping guy, who's following the hairy one carrying the casserole to the tent. "Maybe you can use this," I say, while the young guy smiles, nods, takes the milk in its stiff double bag and says, "Thanks." I know for a fact that young males drink lots of milk.

"And this is from my friend," I say, handing him Nelda's ten dollars while he smiles again and nods. "Keep up the good work," I say. "And stay warm."

"Easier said—," he says, and winks, or something like a wink, a bit frozen, and that's it. I do get a glimpse of some army surplus sleeping bags spread in a jumble across the floor of the tent. A tiny woodstove in the corner. I climb back into the car and pull away behind the woman in the small Chevrolet to begin heading toward Nelda's apartment.

"Nelda," I ask as we settle into a bit of traffic, "do you feel bitter? About your great-grandmother's life? About slavery? Or your dad's life? About injustice in this country?"

"Oh honey," says Nelda, "I'm pretty proud of President Obama. And I figure the past is past. We got to concentrate on now."

"*Amen*," says Aunt Patsy. "Watch your driving, Charlotte. And I do think those young guys should stir their stumps and find *jobs*."

We're all three silent till Nelda says, "Choo, why not take me over to Patsy's so's I can help you carry up these groceries. You and me can wait for Tanya to come, then you can drive me home and get back to your boys. Won't they be home from school about now?"

"Good plan," I say. "OK, Aunt Patsy?" Aunt Patsy nods in agreement, and my mind tosses up a new question. "Listen," I say, "do you two think the urge to nurture others—to *help*—propels us? Helps us all, I mean, or does it impede us? As a species. Not just as women or families or friends—or as nations or whatever." I'm trying to put the thought into words but floundering as I drive. Maybe what I'm really pondering is something else. Something about the nature of power. How do we get it, how do we share it, what is it *really*? Must it be fierce or can it be gentle? But there's no possible way I can ask all that.

Today I had a plan. I'd take Nelda home, then Aunt Patsy and I would head to her condo for the sushi and California rolls I picked up at Safeway. My chance to nurture my aunt a bit. Alone. Which is harder and harder to do with all this elder-alarm stuff. Aunt Patsy loves sushi, and she hates to leave her elderly cat Pickles for more than an hour or two. She adores that cat. Most afternoons when I visit, she and Pickles are asleep in her recliner while Nelda or another caregiver putters around the condo patting at pillows, slicing paper-thin wedges of apple or strips of cheddar cheese to set out like bar favors on the small table beside my aunt's recliner. It's old, a rough log table from her former yard. But I can dig out the sushi right away, I think, or Nelda can, or Tanya, after we carry up the groceries. My mind's busy planning, forgetting my own questions while I pull into the cramped garage at the condo. I'm recalling one other thing, which I say aloud: "Nelda," I say, "do you know that once when I was twenty and very unhappy, Aunt Patsy invited me North to stay with her. I believe that act of generosity changed my entire life."

"Well, I don't doubt it," says Nelda, climbing out of the back seat. Aunt Patsy is wide awake, beaming at us from the front seat while I take her cane and unfold her walker. "But as for your question, Choo, well, a person has to do somethin' with her time, don't she? Or his time. Cain't sit around doing nothin'. Nurturin's good enough, for the mind *and* the body. It's important work. And it's fun sometimes. I don't know about the rest of it—urges and impediments and the species and such."

"Nor me," Aunt Patsy chimes in, wresting the day's power back where it belongs: back to *her*. It's something I've noticed only recently: the subtle power play of seniors, of babies, of the weak. Maybe of love itself. "And I'm getting mighty durned hungry," Aunt Patsy continues, though I suddenly suspect she really means *thirsty*, "while you gals gab."

Cats and Dogs

She wakes in her bed, cold, shivering, alone in the house as always except for the dog—Prince, his warm earthy smell and the puff-puffs of breath rising softly from his space on the carpet beside the bed. But she's thinking of *him*. *Him*, whose name she won't even let herself say anymore, a name she hasn't spoken aloud for years: *him*. Why is she hearing his voice again? *Gravelly as ever. Though he said he's given up cigarettes, didn't he?*

She sits up, wide awake, rubbing her eyes. Why does he always set her reeling like this? Push her into the past. Like falling into a well . . .

~

Years back. Yes, that's what he said when she saw him in Wal-Mart yesterday, the two of them shocked in unison. He—she could read it in the sudden tension of his shoulders, his lips, that tightening at the corners of his eyes while he reached for her hands: still a bit larger than his hands, her terrible mannish hands that she's loved then hated all her life—he was squeezing them in utter shock; she could tell. Though shock always freezes her. Each of them shocked as much by the sight of the other as by the attraction that's still sparking between them. After—*what*? Ten years? Fifteen? More?

Like an actual spark: she's backing away from it a bit, while he steps as always into the arc of the thing, thrusting his chin at her while he talks, while he squeezes her big hands. While he jokes, pulls her to him for a quick, absolutely devastating but somehow necessary and perfectly right hug. In Wal-Mart. Where she almost never shops. Except for the cheap newsprint tablets she's gotten so hooked on lately. *Here*. Himself, still.

"Your voice sounds the same," she says to his soap-smelling neck, into the shoulder of his corduroy jacket. Hard to do since his shoulder is still at the same level as hers. And why is her largish head bending over like this— submissive as ever: *I haven't been submissive, or girlish, for decades, have I?* Why is she leaning against him to speak her idiotic words? Words so damned stilted—just as always: *Words always our thing?* "Exactly the same," she's saying. Like reciting her part in some silly play.

By which inane and useless syllables she of course meant that his voice— like every particle of his aged and otherwise altered self—could still melt her. Stunningly melt her. Absolutely melt her cold, half-dead, fifty-six-year-old heart. Just as cornily, just as surely, as his voice, his being, his entire self, again and again—*always*—melts her. When she was thirty-six, thirty-nine, and on. And how old was he then—all those long years ago? Or now? How old *is* he anyway? Sixty? Older? Or her age? Why has she never known?

But that's when he replied—with a joke, as usual—with the quip about his voice: "No thanks to Camels." Then he'd gone on to tell Marian how he'd given up cigarettes: "Years back." Yes.

$$\approx$$

"During Hannah's chemo," he said. Hannah was his young wife. His young second wife. *Twenty years ago young, of course. Everything tangled in time*: Hannah, a young, beautiful creature with thick honey-colored hair in Marian's mind, in that vivid shard of a memory like a quick-study sketch— pastel rather than charcoal—Hannah had died.

"Winter before last," he said, his eyes betraying something like moisture while he talked on haltingly, slower than usual, clinging to Marian's hands, stepping back from his hug. From *their* hug. Telling Marian about Hannah's third awful round of chemo. The chemo seemed endless, useless, he said. More and more pointless, more and more devastating—but it was during this terrible third round that he'd finally quit smoking.

Marian knew about chemo. "I'm so sorry," she said, meaning it, feeling it. Lars had had chemo too.

"Listen," he said, "we can't talk here. I'm late for a g.d. dental appointment, and I know you've got stuff to do too. Carly's trying to resurrect me. Rehabilitate me, damn her. Tend to my physical being, that kind of crap, starting with my teeth."

Carly was his youngest daughter. Marian remembered Carly. And he'd already half-explained all that: he was staying here in town with Carly. Back in Fairbanks, where he'd grown up, *or tried to*, as he used to love to joke, with mock irony, way back when.

In his forties then? Or still in his thirties, like herself? Why has she never even known his actual age? *What have I ever really known about him, despite it feeling like—everything?*

And his daughter a woman now. A girl as Marian recalls it, a girl only a bit younger than Hannah was when he married her. Carly probably still in her teens that heady spring.

Marian thought all this in one gasp, in Wal-Mart, trying to recall Carly: a big-boned, not-quite-mature blonde girl who looked nothing like her father. Carly glaring suspiciously at Marian the one time they'd actually been in the same room. Or in the same hallway. At the forestry office building, the hallway outside his office. *He's nothing like all these others*, Marian decided right then. As she herself wasn't. One fact she knew.

～

He pulls a marking pen from his pocket to jot a phone number into Marian's left palm. "Call me tomorrow morning," he says while she tries hard to breathe. "Ten or so." Then he'd squeezed her hands and walked deeper into Wal-Mart, not looking back.

～

She's walked the dog, showered, eaten, sketched a bit, when she calls. His voice pours through the line, gravelly but with tenderness hidden—she can feel it; it's still there: "Well, I'm no damned athlete. But—we could walk your dog. Though I'm a cat person. As you know. Parking lot at Carlson Center by the river. Thirty minutes or so. OK."

Marian, overwhelmed by the absolute intensity of him, cannot believe it. *Him.* Again. Her Prince Charming once—*here*—and she places the phone receiver, like a delicate sacred object, back in its cradle and goes to wash the charcoal from her fingers. Though the dark marking pen numbers stay clear and vivid in her left palm.

~

He's late. Marian waits above the footpath, standing above the mostly frozen river with the frisky young dog. Lars' last dog—a medium-sized, shaggy, black-and-white mixed breed who pulls at the retractable lead, bounds into the snowbank, half disappears, then rolls forward, tangling his head in the lead. It's a remarkably warm day for late January, a perfect day for walking, as the dog seems to be saying with every ounce of his body.

Marian calls to the dog softly as she always does, then pats her thigh: *Come.* Which he does immediately for once, while she untangles the lead and retracts it, pets his long head. Takes off her heavy gloves to caress the always-surprising silk of his coat with her bare hands as she loves to do, hunting with the tips of her fingers for the slight retriever bump on the top of his skull bone as always, and the dog sits, just as she commands but tingling with anticipation: "Stay." Marian says it softly, and the dog lets its glossy body relax visibly, just as Lars taught him to do. Always a small, tender, and pleasant shock.

She had not wanted the dog: Prince. Lars named him, another in that long string of cliché pet names they always gave to dogs. Lars chose him, from the pound again, trained him a bit as always, then that long remission went into a spiraling reversal—last spring, not quite a year ago—and all at once it was just Marian and Prince, poking around in the too-big house. She misses Lars. Much more than she could have imagined. She aches with it sometimes: that longing for Lars. It seems, maybe, as if she loves Lars more in his absence than she did in his presence, oddly. She still cannot think of herself as a widow.

Another odd thing is that she's grown to love the dog. Prince feels to her like Lars' last sweet gift, a recompense for their long, not always happy marriage. She'd been neutral to most of their other dogs, as she was to Lars' actual gifts: art books hunted so carefully, and her first good set of acrylic paints. Good used cars carefully chosen just for her. Small boxes of the Danish chocolates she's always been half-addicted to but would never buy for herself. Jade earrings once. And that long series of reading lights, for travel and for reading in bed, which she loves to do: *This woman loves reading in bed more than she loves sex.* Lars used to say that, whispering the familiar words. Then he'd kiss her, nuzzling her left ear, a tender ritual to start off their lovemaking sometimes.

Now she can appreciate it all: Lars' patient, confident love. She'd been busy with the kids when they were small. And with Alaska's climate. And work, why she didn't appreciate things maybe. Then with their grandkids, so busy when they were toddlers—and with plain old life. That most of all, she supposes. She retired the month of her fifty-sixth birthday last September, only five months after the funeral, and now maybe she simply has time to be—but *what?* Fussy? Sentimental? Self-indulgent? Or just herself?

Maybe she never did appreciate Lars. It might be true. She's thinking all that while she waits, with Prince panting beside her. Or appreciate their dogs. This one, she loves.

When a dark navy Volvo appears, the car must be his, not Carly's, Marian's certain. He parks, climbs out slowly. Lars would like this car, she thinks. It's a sedan, oldish but not bad looking, a two-door. Lars might've called it sexy, though Lars never owned one.

He did—*always*, Volvo after Volvo. It's like all the Volvos he always drove. Back when she knew him, at least: *Or thought I did.* Such an odd car for a forestry person: four-wheel drive, but not a truck. One thing she'd liked, admired right off about him when she noticed the first Volvo—*how many years back?*—out in the staff parking lot.

Lars was a Chevrolet man, then Toyotas. Though for a few brief months before the cancer returned, Lars brought Volvo catalogs home, picked up at the dealer's showroom in Anchorage when they drove south through the mountains to visit their sons. Anchorage is where he, and Hannah once, lives, or lived. Marian looked up the phone number in an Anchorage phone book years ago, but she couldn't bring herself to dial. And Prince is up on his feet, alert, staring across the empty, almost snow-free parking lot that lies between herself and him and the Volvo as if it's a territory to be protected: Prince's assignment, a kingdom being invaded. Marian knows the look.

Then comes the deep-chested woof. And another. "No," Marian's saying. "*No!*" She hasn't even thought about this, hasn't once considered it. She *had* wondered if he'd like Prince, how she'd react if he didn't: *But what if Prince doesn't like him?* That notion, for some reason, hasn't until now crossed her mind. Prince is a dog who likes everybody.

"Sit!" she's commanding. And Prince does, unwillingly, still tingling, ready to pounce: she can see it.

"Christ," he says. "This is the dog?" Prince is growling, though very faintly. She's not sure he can hear the growl across that distance. Can he still hear? He's wrapping a thick red scarf around his neck, as if it's much colder out than it really is, while he glances back at the car then walks toward her. Prince tingles in silence, very alert, and she feels almost angry: "He was Lars' dog," she says—too loudly? "I'm—attached to him."

"I can see that," he says, grinning his old grin, nodding toward the retract-able lead. "I guess you walk him around here all the time, huh? Aren't there drunks? Carly says there tend to be obnoxious drunks on the bike path."

Is he making some kind of joke? One of her old hesitations about him had been drink. She knew all the rumors: days he missed work in the forestry office because he was "sick." Quarrels, odd behavior at staff parties, the young women he'd made various silly and ill-timed plays for—when, so the gossip went, he was in his cups. But then, wasn't all that really what she admired? Rebellion against the endless pettiness of everyday life?

"Not so you'd notice," she says. "No. Not in the middle of the day. Anyhow I've got Prince." She's pulled her voice back down to normal range, but her earlobes still burn.

"Prince Charming," he says, uncharmingly, and he chuckles aloud with that dismal, gruff clucking sound she suddenly remembers. It's a sound she'd forgotten but actually hated.

"We don't have to do this," she says. "Walk, I mean. We could go have a cup of coffee. Sit down somewhere." *Why didn't I just invite him up to the house? Hedging my bet as always? It's not as if he's a rapist.*

"I'm slushing with coffee," he says. "Carly's a fiend for coffee despite the health kick. Let's walk." Marian suddenly can't think why she suggested any of this. This specific walk, in her mind, is the best—her favorite in decades of small, possibly boring daily activities she and Lars loved. She decided during the months Lars was dying that this walk was probably the most success-ful—and the most *sensual*—thing they'd done together since they met, in college, in an undergraduate English class Lars loved and she, uncharacteris-tically, hated: walking here, beside the small sleepy river that almost defines Fairbanks. Watching slow canoes or speedboats pass on sun-drenched sum-mer nights, fireworks across the river after the fair in August, darkness returning, set off from the fairgrounds but visible here beyond Pioneer Park. How many times?

And the Red Green Regatta: all those duct-tape rafts filling the river in July, Prince swimming among them, Lars' last summer. And the raft Lars' friends built like a floating painted roof once, the summer after Hurricane Katrina:

STILL WAITING FOR FEMA

All those teenagers leaping off the footbridge into the Chena on hot late nights in July one year, bright light till midnight, so warm out, but faint sun-set painting the bend in the river. Bare-chested boys, drunk probably, and a few girls: shouting, laughing, daring one another to leap for the breath-takingly cold plunge. Something she's always intended to paint but hasn't. Reflections of sky and trees shimmering on the water in fall. More beautiful than reality, more beautiful than anyone's life, really. But *real*, not imagined. She and Lars moving carefully along the icy path in deep winter. All of it like a solemn beautiful dance in her mind. Like lovemaking, her real life: *Why did I suggest this walk?*

"I guess you walk here all the time?" He's repeating it. He's wearing sturdy, heavy shoes, but just shoes; she notices that. Thick soles but no warmth to them. Not boots, not shoepacs, not right at all for even a short walk down the winding snowy path. His feet will be wet, or frozen, in no time. Even the cap's all wrong: just a city cap, not warm.

"Your feet," she says, while he waves a hand dismissively, and she goes on: "Not really. We usually walk in the woods by the house, Prince and I." *Why didn't I just invite him up to the house, for godsakes?*

Prince has stopped growling to sniff his shoes while he stands still, looking down, peering with that slight frown at the dog. In truth, Prince usually runs free in the woods, loping ahead of Marian like a wolf. She feels alone then, and she loves it: carrying the retractable lead in one hand, ambling slowly—and so happily—far behind. She's come to love the tangled trails that cut through the woods by the house: dog tracks and moose trails some of them, others actual old human paths edging her tame yard. A fine kingdom she'd never ventured into in the twenty years in the house. Not until two years ago, when Lars brought Prince home. It was her salvation to walk in the silent woods during the terrible days of Lars' decline, and now again since she's retired: walking every day deep into the woods. It's a safe run for Prince, who loves to run and needs it. Though Lars always preferred this shorter, less demanding downtown walk. Lars didn't mind driving into town for a walk.

She thinks of the two moose she saw browsing below the woodsy trail when she walked there yesterday. Amazing that Prince didn't see them or smell them: their plump, long-legged forms bent away downhill in the snow. Browsing, sometimes stretching their long necks up for the birch stalks. *Half a mile from the house only, but absolutely another world to me. And the amazing hair of the near one's long back legs as it bent to browse: white as silk stockings.* The sort of thing you can't describe in words but can *see*, maybe hope to paint later on. Something to thrill to when you're out walking—well, yes, with a dog.

Prince is growling again, very softly. "Sit!" Marian says. And again, more firmly: "*Sit!*" Her face is flushed red; she can feel it, but why? He doesn't look as if he's afraid of Prince, though maybe he should be: *Should he be?* "Sit!" she's repeating.

~

"He smells Carly's cats," he says, stepping back, moving his feet up and down, stomping lightly in place, while Prince does sit, vibrating, his deep chest shivering. She's taken off her gloves to stroke Prince, hoping for calm—but she knows why she chose this specific walk: it's hers. What she really loves: *humanly social as I care to be.* One among the wild creatures nearly invisible in Fairbanks, animals you only chance on when you give yourself up to their world: *It's my life now—and he'd probably hate it.* Foxes, a lone eagle soaring over the frozen Chena on a walk once. Dozens of over-wintering mallards who swim all winter in the open water from the power plant. Pintails and cranes in warm weather, so many kinds of migrating birds, creatures and scenes she loves completely.

And the beavers. Who could believe those beavers? Though only she saw it in fact.

She'd tried to alert Lars in time: two beavers beside their lodge, each standing upright on its hind legs, face-to-face, embracing. Forepaws on shoulders, head beside head, that quick small bow of a greeting, that cheek rub, then again to the opposite side—the unbelievably civilized greeting of loved ones, cheek to cheek.

Such a gift to see it! Lars followed when she motioned to him, on tiptoe almost, with Prince staying quiet. But Lars was too late. He'd hurried so quickly down the rain-slick beaver path, through the chewed-up raspberries and willows, down one of the slippery and tangled beaver slides she loves. To the edge of the big beaver lodge she named—for Lars—*Sweet Haven*. Like the town in the *Popeye* movie, an American opera really, the old movie their grandkids love. But, yes, too late. She alone had been given that gift.

"Were they mating?" Lars asked that, whispering, panting, when he came close. But no. She'd shaken her head no. Not mating. Just—love. Civility, loyalty, a small familiar ritual, some intimate exchange between equals: the embrace of Europeans wearing sleek beaver coats: *Or like that brief, intense hug—his and mine—yesterday?*

~

And she sees why she loved him back then. She respected him. His intelligence, his wit—*himself*—things nobody else seemed to notice in those days. Except maybe Hannah.

And he felt that. Appreciated it. Once, when he and Hannah had been publicly angry, had broken up for some months, he and Marian stood chatting in the empty break room: *with sparks between us as always.* Though he was by then dating a dark-haired flighty woman Marian knew well, saw as a fool. Marian can't recall how she found courage to say it, but she had: *You know, you're better off with Hannah.* Calm, serious Hannah.

That. When she'd only met Hannah two or three times, at boring parties. He'd stared hard at her: *My Marian,* he'd said, shaking his head; that look of total possession in his eyes; loving her, accepting the truth from her. He'd married Hannah the next year.

She'd always felt he could see right through any attempt she made at a false pose too, as she could his, staring deep into her heart. That one spring—at somebody's wedding, when he'd all at once kissed her while they danced— she thought it might start up her real life, *their* life at last. They'd been surrounded by passion and divorce all that year, in town, at work. But maybe all that was what stopped them? He'd phoned the next day. Apologized. In that year of so many hot and visible schisms, so much sex everywhere, there'd been no lovemaking between them despite his reputation.

Or maybe because of his reputation? He wanted no more dissembling? He had Hannah, she had Lars: Maybe successful players at love require masks: role-shifting, games? *Not the respect-filled recognition I chanced on in the embracing beavers?*

⁓

"What kind of cats does Carly have?" Marian knows it's an inane question. Again.

She's stopped petting Prince, but they haven't moved yet. He's still stomping his light shoes in place. Maybe he and she love only the serious side of the other somehow? Some deeper reality? A hint of the hidden, the least secure but most real self? She saw it in him often back then. In those hopeless, hostile, over-long staff meetings, when he'd give her a quick glance then speak the obvious, bringing all the acidic exchanges back to a focused point, ending the tiresome game. As if he drew strength from that single quick glance they exchanged.

"Heinz 57," he says. *Will they ever begin to walk?* Prince is lying down again but looking ready to pounce. "Hannah's cat's offspring, the third generation."

She remembers it with a pang then. All the awful talk at a party years and years ago, at his and Hannah's apartment, years before they married, though they already lived together, with his kids. Marian barely knew him in those days, it was that long ago: all that talk behind carefully cupped hands, whispers about how he and Hannah had perfected "cat birth control." Tossing litters of live kittens Hannah couldn't find homes for into the dryer. "There *is* such a thing as too many cats," one whisperer said. Marian still wants to believe it wasn't true. Though her own beloved dad *did* drown a litter of kittens in the creek when she was a child. *Maybe I'm too soft for him? Too naïve? Or maybe I've never known him at all?*

"I—I don't think this is a good idea," she says. "Your feet," pointing at them. "And this dog. I'm sorry." Prince is staring up at her, looking wary and puzzled.

He's laughing, that laugh she remembers, the soft, hoarse deepness. That rich manly laugh she loved so helplessly once. "Marian, Marian," he's saying. "You haven't changed a bit, have you? Either. Still my Maid Marian." He's reaching for her big bare hands, caressing them while Prince growls, turning her palm up to look briefly at the inked-in phone number. Still visible, Marian sees with a blush. Once he told her she was the most determined person he'd ever met. Maybe the best compliment anyone's ever given her. Yet so utterly shocking. As if he'd suddenly revealed more about her than she'd ever be able to discover for herself in a lifetime of questing. "Are you still painting?" he asks.

She's nodding. It's true, she is painting. Every day, without Lars. Seriously since she's retired, as if she's found out what her hands are made for. *Work.* Watercolors of the woods. Quick sketches that veer into something more. Rain, fog, snow, wet spring leaves, cranes weaving the sky, sometimes a newborn grandchild. Wildflowers, birds, trees, even moose. Darker things too, charcoal sketches and quick studies that shock her. She's nodding, tears filling her eyes while he squeezes her hands and Prince growls on faintly.

"It's been great, seeing you," he says. He drops her hands, grinning that tender grin she still loves. Smiling really, walking backwards toward the Volvo. Smiling for her a kind of good-bye, then turning away, climbing in, while Prince growls on very softly.

Maybe I'm becoming an artist at last: can it be true? What she's always dreamed of, put off forever, the life she's longed for since girlhood and is still trying to choose: *that bold life set apart that I must have imagined in him—once—so long ago.* And loved.

But it's not something you can choose. It's something you must *do,* must *be*—or not. Like a quick-study sketch. Or like falling in love. She sees it now. She's pulling Prince on his lead toward the Volvo.

"Wait," Marian's calling, "wait!" while he turns his head to look back, scrolls down the window, leans out. She can feel her whole life turning upside down, everything tossed into the air, see it all in that shocked look in his eyes. And there are his books scattered around inside the car. Books everywhere. That defining trait she'd almost forgotten—and loved. Always a slim dog-eared book of poems in his pocket, novels he'd quote from, books of psychology, old classics and new writers he'd speak about in hushed, reverent tones in that gravelly voice she loves.

And she's thinking in words what she's probably always felt: how much like a dog he is somehow: an irrepressible terrier maybe, friendly, lively, optimistic. *And myself like a cat then: quiet, secretive, so pointlessly elegant and aloof?*

"Don't go, Mick," she says softly, her eyes feeling locked on his, his name on her lips like an old song she's known forever. "Let's—walk."

Contagion

Sandy imagines one of the signs as the first. It's half the size of a recipe card, edged with blue flowers and tiny butterflies frozen among a tangle of gilded but greenish faded leaves. Like a preprinted self-stick label or maybe a name tag stuck to the dark wood of the apartment door, it's pasted below a small wreath made of pinkish-orange and pale yellow cloth flowers, and it reads:

> PLEASE REMOVE YOUR SHOES
> BEFORE ENTRY. I HAVE
> ALLERGIES. THANK YOU.

The second sign, next door to its left, is neatly and carefully hand-lettered in shiny black ink and taped slightly higher on its door:

> *Take off your shoes before you*
> *enter, please. Allergies.*

There's a third sign—like a veritable contagion, Sandy thinks; when her grandsons moved into the apartment building, they called this the allergy floor. It's hand-scrawled in black marker on cardboard and it hangs across the hall from the other two:

Unless you WANT TO SCRUB THIS
*FLOOR **TAKE OFF YOUR SHOES***
OUT IN THE HALL-
*WAY. [This means **EVERY-***
***BODY**. EXCEPT MAYBE GIL OR DESIREE.]*

The doormat below this third sign holds a motto, dust-scoured but far larger than any of the others, and it proclaims:

ONE NICE PERSON AND ONE OLD GROUCH LIVE HERE

Sandy, who lives in a suburb and has rarely entered any other apartment building in years, has seen only one person come or go over the motto: a very thin, lively-looking, wiry, and wiry-haired woman with a wry sense of humor.

"I know. Oh yes, I know about all that," the woman's proclaimed to Sandy, waving a hand and grinning while being bumped into (coming off the elevator) by a fast-moving boy half her size. Christopher. Both Eddy and Matt move more slowly. (Chris, fearing Sandy's wrath, may have called back over his shoulder, "Oops. Sor-rry," though Sandy isn't certain.) "Plenty of that in my time. I know, I know," said the woman.

Is she a decade (or two?) older than Sandy? Is she Tlingit? Or maybe a remarkably skinny Yup'ik? The last of some nearly vanished Alaskan tribe?

Not Athabascan, Sandy thinks. The woman's humor swells up in a way that suggests craggy mountains and hard coastal rains. Or else the flat frozen expanse of an ocean's edge out the kitchen window six months of the year, winds more fierce than anything known to the Interior. But maybe she (like Sandy) is atypical? Untouched by the forces of home? Is she the nice person or the grouch? Or both rolled into one, like Sandy herself these days? Sandy can't decide.

Sandy's own apartment, technically, belongs to her son and his sons. But she secretly regards it as at least in part her own. It sits at the far end of the hallway, two doors beyond the nice person and grouch, on the right-hand side too. Between them comes the home of another newcomer: long-haired, tallish and trim, dark-eyed and kind-faced, a quiet-looking Athabascan person, a head-dipping young woman. Shy or perhaps not easy with words in a way that Sandy, who likes Athabascans and has lived most of her life among them in the wintry center of Alaska, does see as typical. This woman is her son's age and Sandy must admit to having (as she has for nearly all the unattached young women in the apartment complex) a few designs. For her son's sake: this woman might make both a good wife and mother. So far Sandy's seen her only once or twice.

Across the hall from the shy woman live Alexander and his wife or companion: Russians, clearly recent émigrés, in their seventies Sandy guesses. Alexander—a retired photojournalist, her son says—is wiry as the nice person/grouch, and (while hunting coins, doing his-and-her laundry on Tuesday mornings) he speaks a tortured and brief English. His lady, apparently, none. Though she nods eloquently and smiles and smiles when Sandy tries, occasionally, to apologize in English for the herd of three small boys racing ahead downstairs—to their bikes, to the park. Once Sandy said, as distinctly as possible, "Spasiba," thanks.

One of her proud handful of Russian words spoken clearly as she could manage while Alexander and his lady stood aside. Not exactly pressed to the wall, but, well, they do tend to carry themselves—or at least Alexander does—like a carton of eggs. This brief multicultural exchange took place as Sandy raced past in the hallway following the boys. Though neither neighbor seemed to understand. Perhaps they can't hear well?

The boys make a contrast to the other residents. Including Sandy, who finds herself often short-tempered or short of breath, though she doesn't ever, or hardly ever, miss her real life. There's no time! Anyway, it waits, she knows, 365 highway miles north in Fairbanks—a day's drive through the mountains.

The boys stop sometimes to talk to people (who often cannot or do not understand).

Though the two young teachers—unmarried, female, pretty; Sandy can't help having her designs—who live together in the apartment below her son and grandsons, *do* joke and banter a bit with the boys. As do the ponytailed mailman and the (various, coming and going) plumbers and cleaning women and apartment managers who've been here, on and off, in and out, during the last two hot, summery months.

Sandy sleeps on an inflatable mattress (the boys love to pump it up and deflate it) on the living room floor. With her teacup of cool water beside her, her book (or books, or *Harper's* magazine) and her fold-up alarm clock (which the boys are too mature this summer to admire) and the very small boudoir lamp with a silk pleated shade (for reading), which her son found for her at one of the thrift stores he loves, all carefully placed beside her dark blue mattress on the carpet—well, *then*, nights, she feels cozy and, yes, serene: queen-like, at rest on an airy cloud. As if this is the best yet of the many roles so far in her life. She feels at home.

As she does sometimes carrying a plastic grocery sack filled with peanut butter sandwiches (or salami, the favorite this week), jog/stumbling along Chester Creek breathless behind the boys. Trying to keep up, shouting to them to get over to one side and to watch out for oncoming joggers—or bikes or tricycles or dogs or street people. To stay out of the creek, and don't ride bikes straight into the woods—and to wait up. To meet her at the playground at Valley of the Moon Park.

Or, as she does very late at night (now that it's begun to be dark again) with everyone else asleep, Sandy herself standing on tiptoe on an arm of the living room couch looking west out the top of the picture window toward Arctic Boulevard. For the illuminated, transparent gold onion domes of St. Nicholas of Myra Byzantine Catholic Church glowing faintly in the pale night sky. *If Anchorage, Alaska, can be Heaven*, she's thinking, knowing the absurdity of this thought, *I am there now.*

Human Being Songs

The girl's voice was sweet and pure—intoxicating to Rena, like a spirit calming the sea:

> *The wind doth blow today, my love,*
> *And a few small drops of rain—*
> *I never had but one true love,*
> *In a cold grave he was lain—*

It was New Year's morning, damp and chill, and Rena stood out of the wind; intent, shivering, huddled among a handful of people clumped together in a stairwell watching the street musicians. There were two bearded men and the girl, harmonizing, swaying, the girl now tapping her foot while they began a bawdy Irish drinking tune Rena could not endure. Not after the other.

But why had the girl's song moved her so? Left her suddenly feeling so lost. Bereft. Rena daubed at her eyes with a thumb, ignoring the new tune while she blinked away salty tears—but why? Were the tears somehow for her own life—or for the girl's, as they seemed to be? But what could she possibly know of the girl's life?

Ah yes, of course. Tears. The human lot. Hers and the girl's, every soul's lot. But what a thought! Another sign of her own aging? *Rena Huzar, you are a fool*, she thought, and she squared her plump shoulders and began hunting in her coin purse, hoping to find a dollar bill. When she could not find one, she took out a quarter instead, her largest coin, and stepped forward to drop it into a coffee cup set up beside the girl's tapping sandal.

As Rena bent—careful, leaning under the girl's scrolled metal hand harp: what was it called? a dulcimer maybe?—her eyes caught a flicker of pale skin. A hole in the girl's argyle sock, just under the pad of her big toe. Then, far above on a curve in the long cement stairwell, there was a blink of her daughter's bright green jacket and Celia herself, turning away, kneeling, Celie's beautiful head thrust forward to take a snapshot with her cell phone—a slice of Elliott Bay, pearly in the damp morning light.

In this dull light Celia glowed like an angel. Amazing to think that Celia was her own child. Neither of her daughters seemed to Rena anything like herself. Celie was as quiet as she is, and serious, but bold in ways that puzzled Rena. Beautiful too. Delicate, fine-boned, tall. Opposite in every physical dimension from herself, though with dark hair and fair skin like her own. And a tall homeless man passed by, cut off the view, cradling a tiny dog to his chin. *How do you know the homeless? But you do*, she thought; she does.

Marilynne, her older girl, was stocky and plain. Nearly as short and thick as Rena, but with something Phil always saw as style. Even as a child Marl was flamboyant, and she's clearly a rebel still, at twenty-six. Though with no simple focus for her rebellion. *Just—everything*, Rena decided again. Wild hair, tattoos, several piercings in each earlobe—and the cats. Or like wearing that sari for a wedding gown. And marrying Royce.

"Hurry, Mom." Certainly Celie's voice, and Rena tried to climb the damp stairs more quickly. Walking uphill these days winded her. "Old lungs protesting," her own mother might have said, though Rena's feet felt weightless without boots. Without snow!

Rena and Celia had come to Seattle for Marl's wedding and soon—in a few hours—they'd be flying home to Anchorage, with Rena trying hard to ignore the pangs of loneliness for Marl that began last night. Even before she and Celie said their good-byes and stood waiting in the doorway at Marl and Royce's apartment building, waiting for a cab to carry them back downtown to the hotel. Celie had insisted on waiting outside for the cab, being, she said, sick of aural sex: Royce and Marl's ear nibbling. So they'd wasted nearly half an hour shivering on the doorstep to faint sounds of unseen fireworks. On New Year's Eve!

They'd been half-angry at one another too, though it did seem right to leave the newlyweds alone. And they had after all been forewarned. Marl and Royce explained months ago that they preferred not owning a car in Seattle, preferred taking buses or cabs, or walking, bicycling, and so could not offer rides. Part of the artist's life, Rena supposed.

At home in Anchorage she does not miss Marilynne. It's here, last night, leaving the tiny apartment. Watching Marl dip her shoulders toward Royce as they spoke their good-byes, hugging Marl again, then wandering today, without Marl, through darkened Pike Place Market, the stalls closed for New Year's Day. All that makes Rena ache.

It isn't that she disapproves of Royce; she told herself that again. She is *not* a racist. His dark skin, *race*, worries her far less—she repeated this to herself, too—than the fact that he has no thought of a real job and still, at thirty, wears his long kinky hair pulled back with a rubber band. Even at his own wedding! Well, the rubber band alone would've made Phil hoot!

But then Marl must be like her father in this too, as with her coloring and personality: choosing an offbeat mate. Phil's family disapproved of Rena, still. The Huzars all saw her as prim and dull, dreamy, unworldly: *useless*. Which she is *not*! But these words renamed exactly what Phil said from the start he loved in her, found so very "exotic." He'd called her, always, "Birdie" or, sometimes, half-joking, "my nestling."

But Celia was waving her forward again, mouthing the words, "Hurry, Mom, please!"

While Rena waved back, panting, trying to smile, her eyes still full of Marl.

Marilynne is no nestling, Rena decided. She's short and full-figured as Rena, yes, but with slanted eyes and that strong ironic voice, like Phil's. Dusky skinned as he'd been too, and with pale sandy hair the same color and exact thick, wild, nearly kinky texture that was standard for everybody in Phil's family. Hair nearly as wild as the woman's passing by now, wearing layer on layer of ragged dirty coats. Marl seemed part of some inexplicable new breed: people who *flaunt* failure. Like the street singers. Clearly Marl cares nothing—as Celie does—for conventional achievement. But is Marl's rebellion only a form of play? What will take on weight in her life? *What matters for her?* The real question.

Rena felt certain the strange art Marl and Royce make—rude dabs on ugly gray canvas—was not serious work. Marl herself was perpetually disheveled. As she'd been all her life, of course: sloppy, messy beyond mere shabbiness, though she loves bright colors and odd clothing, just like Phil's mother and sisters. Hungarian gypsy in the blood, *Hunky style*, Phil called it, joking at the old ethnic slur. So opposite to the simplicity and reserve he claimed to love in Rena. What'll become of Marl? What will life hold for her?

And for Rena herself? Can she open her heart to mixed-race grandchildren?

But what a question! Yet one she pondered often. And pushed away: *Of course I'll love any child of Marl's.* But how would Phil have taken it? Would he approve? Rena supposed—not. Not at first, at least. Still, as he often said: *Pick your battles. Don't interfere.* Phil was no tyrant. And look at their own life. Parents' approval meant so little, really.

And she does respect Marl's lifelong sense of herself. That conviction. *Strength.* The small pudgy hand remaking her name: *MARL* scrawled in crayon everywhere when she was three. *MARL* on all the doorjambs and half the walls of the house. Marl had renamed Celia to Celie, too.

But there was the ache again. That Phil didn't live to see their girls step forward to enter their adult lives. *Marriage!* Marl and Royce were both potters as well as painters, and Marl was teaching a pottery course this year at the university. Phil would've been proud of that, just as she is. Glad for Marl's happiness too. And now two obese street persons! Young men. Twins? Why is life so strange? And so unfair? Phil should have lived to see—but what? Well, maybe to see Celia so beautiful. So scholarly and self-assured, and so *focused!* Already making plans for her master's degree at twenty!

"I've asked around," Celia said, reaching for Rena's hand as they threaded their way through more street people. They seemed to be everywhere, nothing like the street people at home, the ones who practically live outside the shop. Failure seemed sharper here. Maybe the thickly peopled world cut at you more readily? Failure as cutting, as biting, as this cold wind. But there was a sense of raw energy too. "It's not far, Mom. Seven blocks or so," Celie said.

The Rack, she meant, Nordstrom's discount store. Celie insisted on checking out of the hotel early, leaving their suitcases at the desk, so there'd be time to shop. A trip to Seattle, for Celie, meant not her sister's wedding or a family visit but an avid hunt through The Rack for clothes. Something she'd done only twice before—when she was thirteen, on the advice of a classmate, then again after a year in France as an exchange student, at seventeen. And the wind was awful! Worse by far than Anchorage wind.

"Keep in mind that I'm broke," Rena said. While Celie patted her hand: "When aren't you broke, Mom? I have money."

Phil died of leukemia four long winters ago. Two years before Celia left for France. Celie so young to leave home—still nearly a child, a high-school exchange student—but she'd returned a young woman. So quiet and self-assured, no longer a mere girl. Phil missed that transformation too. He did see September 2001, of course—9/11, years ago. Better to have been spared that? The familiar world transformed: not just all the changes to travel, but the flag-waving craziness; endless war and real terror, even in Alaska.

Phil was the one who'd loved Alaska. Rena grew tired of the winters and the distance long before his illness, and his final terrible year confirmed things. But now she couldn't leave. Couldn't sell the shop—Arctic Collectibles—her rock in a storm, crammed with dusty books, old tools, souvenirs, and minor northern artifacts. How could she let go of a life's work given over to such eccentric hoardings? Or give up downtown Anchorage, "hunkered amongst the drunks," as Phil loved to joke, calling it street theater.

And Celia was squeezing her hand: "Three hours till the boarding check, Mom." Celie glanced up from her watch. She'd drawn that green line around her eyes again, below the dark lace of her lashes. More like Marl's East India look than her own delicate style, Rena thought. And Celie bent into the wind, moved with the crowd, forward, away.

But I can give it up, Rena told herself, trudging behind Celia's bright-green jacket. *It's just a matter of making up my mind to sell—even at the loss I'll take on the shop. And on the house—I can!* Maybe she should have planned this wedding trip as part business? A chance to hunt low-priced new stock: bars of black Russian soap, old books, hand-painted trinkets, badly tanned Asian pelts. And not just things to make money from tourists, but some larger and more nebulous quest—a way to acknowledge the dignity of odd objects: *So maybe I do still love the shop?*

A passing girl's sweatshirt read *TAKE HEART,* amidst a cluster of Valentine candy hearts, and Rena smiled. *This summer,* she'd told herself that all morning, long before the other girl's sad song. This summer she'd actually clean up the shop and sell! But then what? Move to Seattle with Celia? Yes! Even if it meant taking a loss on everything. She might even move here alone, if Celie insisted on staying at UAA. She'd escape.

But from *what?* Celie stopped, turned, reached for Rena's hand, squeezed it again: "Are you OK, Mom? Are you hungry? You look pale." Rena shook her head. "We could stop now," Celie said. "Or we can grab a bite at the airport if you'd rather wait. Whenever you're hungry," while Rena nodded. Celie smiled, dropped her hand, moved ahead in the wind, and Rena felt it again, that familiar emptiness food cannot fill. She would not get hungry.

"Let's just head over to The Rack," she answered to Celia's bright back, Celie turning slightly, nodding, smiling that oddly maternal smile. So that Rena felt resigned to her fate: *the dratted Rack.* She felt calm too, ashamed in the midst of all this genuine failure—and all this bustling life!—to be so self-absorbed. Why was she being such a fool?

Maybe around noon she'd dig out the new cell phone she hates and call Marl before they fly home. She was all at once feeling that pang of loneliness for Marl again. But why? Before even leaving Seattle! It'd been years since Marl lived at home. And Royce is a sensitive-seeming man, very gentle. Intelligent too. And he's humorous, always joking in that rich bass voice—a voice so like Phil's. A quirky sense of humor too, like Phil's.

At the wedding two days ago, she'd liked his mother. Also a widow, tall, sturdy, quiet, seemingly as puzzled by the event as herself. At one point Royce's mother took Rena aside: "As a boy, Royce loved cats." She'd begun with half-whispers, shaking her head, then grinning. "I just wanted to tell you that, don't know why. Even as a boy, Royce had more patience and affection for cats than any human I ever did know. He even taught one cat to do tricks! Roll over and smile and such—Royce called it smiling anyways. And to follow him around like a dog. To the playground—that cat went of its own volition, I swear! Free will! It did seem so. He'd even cook for a cat!" And they'd both laughed. "I mean, oh, I don't know. Beyond—oh, art and such—he's not like his dad. Nor me, I guess. I never knew *anybody* who'd cook up scrambled eggs for a cat!"

Royce's mother squeezed her hands just as Celia is doing today. Rena squeezed back, then gave Royce's mother a hug. Their eyes had teared up too, and they'd stood back from one another a while, holding hands, laughing a bit, while a cat eyed them haughtily.

"I know, I know," Rena had said. "Marl too. I know *exactly* what you mean."

But what *did* she mean? What had either of them meant? That Royce was his own distinct person, as Marl was? That he loved Marl and would devote himself to her? That Marl might be a perfect wife for such an odd or gifted man? All of that—or none of it?

And this wind was making her eyes tear up again. Not emotion really: *wind*. Even in a big-city crowd, the wind seemed to seek her out and focus on her. *Madness!* Maybe what she needed most was to get out of this crowd. Anchorage is a city too, but not like this.

Or maybe I just need sex? To get laid? Phil would say that, and Rena grinned then blushed, thinking it. How odd to have sex exist in your life as something in your mind. With a dead—but with my *husband*. My dead husband. Who was—*human*. No saint.

The streets were not nearly so crowded as they were yesterday before supper: the four of them—she, Marl, Royce, Celia—joking about the dregs of Seattle grunge: copied from standard Alaska gear, certainly—while they edged past tables spread with tie-dye, pottery, pyramids of winter vegetables, ice cream, pie shops, coffee houses, kites. Jam or card vendors, fish stands, weavers' stalls. People everyplace, wandering through small exotic sites that smelled of tea or sandalwood, odd spices she could not name. Those tiny stalls dark now, empty, closed for the holiday, but the windy street still full of grunge. The economy. Like home, though maybe it's worse here.

But maybe her sadness was only that? Jitters about the world? Or these street people—how they predominate? How panhandlers and beggars become so visible once the shops close? They accost you everywhere, or sit with their signs and cups spread out on the sidewalk, their feet in the pathway like the girl perched in front of the bookstore, no older than Celia, holding her pathetic cardboard sign like a shield from the wind, with a wooden bowl at her side:

OUT OF WORK AND STRANDED
PLEASE DONATE SO I CAN RENT A ROOM

Rena gave two dimes and a Canadian penny. All she could find in her coin purse except for the twenty-dollar bill she'd need for traveling. Or to put toward boarding Purry, thin elderly Purrina, the family cat.

Hah! *Family* indeed! Was there such a thing as *family* anymore in her life? Celia works in a coffee shop and is rarely home anymore. And there it was: her own sadness again. Nestling with no nest. But anyway—maybe she still believes them all. Believes every beggar and hand-lettered sign in the soft-headed way Phil scoffed at, saying it was just a business, like their own in a way, but calculating. "They're con men, Birdie," he'd said once on a trip here to Seattle—but when? Long before his diagnosis.

But then why were they so thin? So dirty and sick-looking, most of them. Too frail and shabby to be fake. It troubles her today, still, as it always has. Half her life, at least, has she feared and dreaded poverty? But why? Her parents, both poor as kids, had joked about the Great Depression, only sometimes breaking down in embarrassed tears when the topic went deeper. Grandma would not speak of "the hard times," as she called them. Not at all—though the rest of her life was a source of oft-repeated, richly recalled tales Rena had loved once. Still loves, in fact. Money really seemed no part of it.

Anyway, Phil didn't object the summer they opened the shop. Eighteen years ago! How hard to imagine that! He'd said not a word when she baked cookies for the street people who shuffled past on the sidewalk. They were lost-looking Natives, transplants from the bush mostly. Alcoholics, so you didn't dare give them money. Anyway, they didn't beg. But she'd baked a big batch of granola and chocolate-chip cookies, the healthful recipe Marl and Celie loved at the time, and kept the cookies in a glass jar near the door to offer in a friendly way when the chance came.

The chance hadn't come. She'd tried, but there'd been no possible way. She'd seen by their eyes how far off she was. They lived in a world she could not enter so casually, certainly not with a cookie. Though some of them—old Harry and Kaska and a few others—did come around to shovel the sidewalk with Phil, six dollars an hour, that winter.

And most winters since—working with her now, old friends in a way. If they went into jail for a while and dried out, sometimes they brought her carvings they'd made to offer for sale in the shop. Beautiful walrus ivory jewelry and small carvings, or baleen. Strange that jail could bring out a person's latent talents. She was sighing to herself about that as she trudged into the wind, trying to keep Celia's green coat in sight. Thinking that she *does* do practical things, tries to help the street people, gives to the food bank often. But no one can predict what might matter in a human life.

How enormously different her own life is, for example, from the lives of her mother and grandmother, the two women she knew and loved best. Aside from Celie and Marl, of course, who are—how hard to keep it in mind—*women* now. Women moving into worlds and times certain to be even more puzzling than her own young years.

Or maybe just more exciting? Marl would surely say that, possibly also Celia. Yet a new—and poorer?—century did seem unlikely to change life, really. Not its essentials.

"May you live in interesting times," as the Chinese curse put it. Thinking that made Rena smile again. How could it not be a blessing? But her own mother would've found it a curse—fearing travel as she had, hating to leave Tulsa. Mom only came to Alaska once.

And the bedbugs! In the cheap hotel Rena stayed in on her visit here last summer. But why had she thought of that terrible incident now? She's never told Marl or Celie. What a month, afterwards! Amazing that she still loves traveling—and loves to fly. She's truly never feared flying. Or terrorists. Still loves the thrill of travel.

Maybe that's because time and place *do* mean so much? Even this Seattle sidewalk carries some subtle difference in the attitude it requires of you. Coaxes or extracts, flirts and seduces, maybe. One's heart feeds on *place*, like the old ballads—the girl's song. Strange, but true. Some major difference blows at you here, in this wet wind, a mood completely different from Anchorage.

So many street people at home are Alaska Natives for one thing. Athabascans, Yup'iks, Iñupiat, or Tlingit—and only a few here. Thinking this complicated her feelings again. At home, among those calm-looking aboriginal faces, she sometimes felt guilty. Almost crudely busy. Flighty, hasty, superficial, part of an aggressor race. Though she resisted such thoughts as racist: an injustice against herself, an Obama supporter! She hasn't consciously hurt or enslaved anybody, and she is *not* a racist.

But here she's only a tourist. Not responsible. An observer, a motherly stranger. Or—oddly for someone whose business earns so little money—a newly arrived rich person. Foreign in every way, as lost as these wind-ridden street people. And maybe she likes that? Here her sadness can widen, honestly, to include herself. Re-form into compassion for the way time and circumstance can pass anyone by: *My own pity party? But no, larger than that. It's human compassion, isn't it?*

And there was Celie, standing still, shaking her head, holding it to one side quizzically, and frowning. Rena realized that she'd stopped walking: maybe after dropping coins in the stranded girl's bowl? Celia was navigating the sidewalk towards her anyway, signaling with her eyes, then grinning gently, patiently, as you might at a child, and Rena hurried guiltily forward.

"Mom," Celie whispered when she reached Rena—by cutting past two grimy young men who asked for a dime for coffee, while Rena frowned and tried to look, well, *competent*. Yes, that. Maybe it would come to *that* before long? Trying to disguise my mental failings? Rena shook her head firmly "no" to the nearer young man, partly for Celia's benefit. Though she had not one coin left.

And, from Celia: "You look like a lost waif, Mom. Let's stop in the newsstand and get out of this wind for a while, shall we? OK? Warm up a bit?"

The newsstand for Celie meant magazines and newspapers from France, which, though she couldn't read them, Rena loved too. Just touching them—or the ones from Japan, Africa, Australia—even Russia, back in the world again. The former *CCCP*, as she and Phil used to joke, each of them able to say a few Russian words and transliterate bits of the Cyrillic alphabet. So many Russians in Alaska these days! They too, like these foreign newspapers, offered a sense of that larger universe to which Rena knows she belongs, truly if secretly, rather than the fixed and simple unsophisticated dot in space—that plump and widening postmaternal blob maybe?—which she embodied in reality.

But she can't even pretend to read today: her mind is too full, too busy! And soon enough, Celia was as lost in *Le Monde* as Rena had been herself, on the sidewalk near the stranded girl, minutes ago.

Rena moved slowly back toward the sidewalk. Her mind seemed to enter the past again: Maybe Phil saw her cookies that summer as something like protection money—though more likely he saw them only as customarily naïve. As usual, he'd had the loving good sense to keep quiet. He'd let her free-cookie experiment fail without comment. He'd accepted it too when she began, gradually, obviously, to treat old Harry and Kaska and a few others as friends. Dear friends. Phil accepted it all patiently, though he continued to seem to view them as something like minor enemies—competitors, a nuisance, bad for business, nearly foes. A mild encroachment maybe, or a threat. Things beyond his control.

But maybe *that* was the central difference in their personalities, their views of life? Phil believed in control. Which—she saw it clearly now—was why she must sell the shop. He was gone, and she was no businesswoman: she had no urge to control anything.

But how had Phil's toughness worked in their marriage? Was it the trait that permitted her softness? A crutch? If so, how could she in good conscience *not* begin to stand up for herself at last. She *can't* cast off her own stance in the world, her own truth. She can't just give up and sell the shop! Nothing to do with control. Or business or money. Just—*self.*

And there she was, her mind wandering again! A thousand miles from Marl and Royce and Seattle. Even from Celia and all these foreign newspapers.

But this recurring sense of separateness from Celie while standing a few feet from her made Rena think again of something else. Some other time, yet here, but when?

Of course. That family trip here for Christmas years ago.

They'd had only two days in Seattle then flown on to British Columbia. Vancouver, which was their real destination—a European, Asian, and American northern city, in Canada. That was how Rena still thought of it, the reason she'd planned that specific journey, that small vacation. She'd wanted Marilynne and Celia to see a bit of the world, a larger and grander world than the frontier edge they all knew in Alaska. A wider world than they saw when they visited her family in Tulsa, or Phil's in the hilly suburbs outside Pittsburgh. Both in fact so very nearly the same. Startlingly similar. Both so middle-class, so neatly contained and suburban somehow, if you considered it. Anchorage, too.

But, oddly, Vancouver was too. The same. Part of some known map of the world. The civilized or tamed world. All were similar in some subtle way. Though at least the residents of Vancouver spoke more languages than she'd ever heard spoken in one place before in her life: French, Italian, Bengali, German, Chinese, and that wonderfully crisp British English, as well as the familiar U.S. and Canadian versions.

They'd all enjoyed it, neon signs in Chinese in Chinatown, and staying in that cozy, inexpensive family apartment at the Sylvia Hotel. Such a charming old place, covered with leafless wintry vines—and they'd afforded it all easily. Part of her plan, since the exchange rate was so good that year. Yet they'd been isolated from one another through that whole week too. Always together, yet estranged, just as she felt again and again with Celia now. And with Marl and Royce—all week long.

They'd quarreled every day. Mostly over walking, since Phil refused to rent a car. He didn't want to navigate strange city streets in a car he didn't know. It was his vacation too. And Rena's driving, even at home, put him on edge. The girls hadn't wanted to walk, blocks and blocks, everywhere, through snowy slush—wearing everyday shoes. Weather they'd brought with them from Alaska, everybody said: Vancouver residents, in various languages. They hadn't dressed for such weather, expecting—everybody said it at home—that Vancouver would be so much warmer than Alaska. And everybody in Vancouver had said yes, so much snow that time of year was a great rarity.

Only Celia wanted to see the Polar Bear Swim, as she did. "The plunge," locals called it. Phil and Marl considered it corny, that crowd of people outside their hotel on New Year's morning racing down for a dip in English Bay in the snow. Many of them wore costumes—paper sack bears, aluminum-foil spacemen. It was apparently the traditional way to start a new year in Vancouver—far better than a hangover, Rena said, while Phil hooted: "How do you know they don't have hangovers, Birdie? They all look cotton-mouthed to me."

Celie was as eager as she was to see it, and they'd tried. But the crush of people—crowds far worse than here—kept them from getting close, from seeing anything really. Late that night, full of frustration with her family—stretched out in front of the TV in their small suite, snacking, staring with glazed eyes at an American sitcom—she'd left in disgust and walked the few blocks to English Bay in the dark. Unafraid, a tourist after all. Safe. She'd taken her shoes off and waded—alone—into the dark, frigid water.

She hadn't told any of them. But yes, there she'd stood. No costume, her thin wet shoes clutched in her hands, just a few feet out, only a few moments in time, but, yes, promising herself that this small walk into *ocean*—not really a plunge maybe, but an entry—would be her entrance into a larger life. Into water that flowed everywhere on the planet. That small plunge was her promise: a new and grander habit of living. That was her thought at the time, a wider world and its blessing.

She hadn't felt the slightest tug from her real future. That was the irony of it. That Phil would be diagnosed that year and then slowly die. Or quickly, if you thought of an entire life—and terribly. The Known World would continue to move ever more deeply into war and terror, then find itself broke. Which was the way of things, in her experience at least.

It was what she had in common with these street people maybe. And the ones at home—it came to her suddenly: *why* she felt so lost. For she'd left the newsstand and stepped back out onto the sidewalk while Celia read on in *Le Monde*. She did not own her life either, she didn't plan her destiny as so many people she knew seemed to do—or think they might do. She couldn't control any of it, and she knew that. Like these street people? Fatalists too? Accepting fated lives as she did?

So maybe she'd never flaunted possible failure like Marl, or courted future success like Celia, for that single reason—a foreknowledge? A sense of reality opposite to the one that prevails now? She didn't do things, things just happened to her, and maybe it would always be that way in her life? Just as her own and Phil's daughters, whom she'd happily sheltered in her womb, then reared patiently and so carefully—with such love—were not like her at all. Now suddenly—far too suddenly!—they were women. Almost strangers. A thought not so much surprising or even frightening as—*isolating*. Proof that one is indeed an island? *Why* her mother hadn't enjoyed traveling, maybe? The clear views of life it gave? Insights both inevitable and stunning.

Or like marrying Phil when she was twenty, after knowing him only two months. Which seemed to be such a bold step at the time, but had turned out—as she'd soon understood—to be simply fate. Not courage, but their happy fate. Their life. Lovers' luck for once, but simply and only fate.

Or like moving to Anchorage and opening the shop they'd dreamed of for years and then begun—she, at least—to be sick of. Amazing to think that the shop that now held her hostage had been her dream too. Not just Phil's.

Or Phil's dying, her helplessness within it all. Every bit of it was mere chance, beyond any New Year's resolution, beyond money, truly beyond anyone's control—

And a tall, burly, deep-voiced young man was talking to her now. A Northwest Indian, she could tell. Not quite the same stock as at home—though how could a person know such a thing? Similar maybe, but bigger, heavier, softer:

"Could you spare me a dollar to buy some breakfast?" He spoke softly, politely, so gently, his eyes looking deep into hers. Sober, intelligent eyes she seemed to know. Kind, talk-filled, complex, the eyes of an old friend.

"Oh, I'm sorry," she said, bending away from the wind, towards him. "I'd really like to, but I don't have any money to spare."

"Well, that's OK," he said, "don't you be sorry." And he was grinning, a big open and friendly grin, wagging his finger at her, his free hand touching her elbow. "Don't you feel bad now, it's OK. You just be happy, have a fine new year, and don't you feel sorry."

She was staring up at him like a fool, nodding then smiling—though hot tears welled up in her eyes, and she didn't know why. Since she suddenly did feel—well, yes, *miserable*. And *free*! Free to feel that way at last, why not? Her own feelings, by God! Which she has a right to! Feelings he'd somehow released. Given back to her with his generous New Year's blessing.

She was smiling, accepting the full force of his blessing as he backed away, still grinning at her so gently: he surely far richer today than she. Richer in spirit. Able to give of that spirit. She remembered it then, as she watched him turn away. That other new year's blessing—from Celia, years ago. The spray-painted bit of graffiti they'd seen everywhere in Vancouver during that long-ago New Year's trip.

Celia secretly carved it into the waist-high snow mounded beside the driveway at home, there in the front yard when they finally made it back to Anchorage. Surprising them all, making the whole trip a joy again, worthwhile again. Just as that snowy drive did, driving across the gorgeous stretch of land between Vancouver and Seattle. They'd been racing to catch their plane in Seattle after a snowstorm forced the cancellation of all flights in and out of Vancouver, closing down the airport.

Yes, there they'd been. First the cheerful Pakistani cab driver bringing them safely across snowbound and foggy Vancouver, leaving them at the airport in triumph—triumphant themselves too, to have arrived. Making it to the airport, and on time! Then, suddenly stuck among all those other lost and dejected travelers—stranded, all planes in or out of Vancouver down. Until they'd decided, at Marl's suggestion, to rent a car and simply drive to Seattle. Why not? They knew snow.

So they'd done it. They'd rented a car and been blessed by the trip. It had turned out like so many other happy accidents in life: a memorable thing, a triumph. One thing they'd all ended up enjoying completely. That drive through shifting fog and snow—her family, Phil and Marl and Celie and herself, traveling together—for the last time, as it turned out. In that rented car north of Seattle, only miles from here. Phil still hardy and well, driving; herself and Marl and Celia navigating—from a map the rental car agency handed out. All of them laughing together, glad for their passports. Gliding along below snowy mountains, joking, eating chips, singing Christmas carols and hip-hop tunes supplied by Marl while ridges, valleys, and farms filled the car windows, scenes as cheery as Christmas cards or folk paintings, beautiful even to Alaskans—till they got to Seattle: its airport down too.

But—yes, what life really could be. Then Celie's gift to them all when they finally reached home after another day and night, stranded in the SeaTac airport: that line of cookie-cutter figures carved into the snowbank in the driveway. Thick, stylized human forms, hand-in-hand, secretly cut into the snow. With Celie's neat schoolgirl lettering stretching below the linked hands, each round face holding that wide crooked *O* of a human mouth in song—the graffiti image spray-painted everywhere, on walls and underpasses all over Vancouver that lovely, snowy New Year. A benediction, blessing rather than scar:

Rena's eyes were overflowing as she thought of it. What she needed maybe, as the kind young man intuitively knew? Tears? Just as Phil used to tell her: *Go ahead, Birdie—don't hold back. Have yourself a good cry.* Phil's tender face with its absolute gentleness always making her laugh just when she might have felt at her worst. Bringing things back into perspective, curing everything.

And she was hunting in a pocket for a Kleenex when she found it. Because at first it did feel like a Kleenex. Exactly: wadded up, softened and crushed by human fingers—a faded and worn dollar bill!

But where? How? Ah—of course. A minute ago, touching her elbow. Those friendly eyes. Someone from home after all—an Alaskan too. An Aleut or a Kuskokwim Delta Yup'ik? A heart that wide. Someone from home, the young man—he'd stuffed it into her pocket—an Alaskan after all.

She was smiling, nearly laughing, waving at Celia to hurry, eager to tell her, when it all reversed again. For months after, for years maybe—she could feel it coming on—she'd replay this scene in her head. Ponder the questions flooding her mind, clamping her heart.

Why did she need to believe somebody gave her the dollar? Couldn't it simply have been there all along? Her own money? Change stuffed into her pocket during harried bits of snack shopping yesterday, here? Or last night, as she and Celie climbed, exhausted, from the cab?

But if so, why didn't she find it and give it away as she'd wanted to do? Why not? Thwarting herself again. Why were her feelings only fresh and alive when somebody else—someone so opposite from herself, as Phil was— or the street singer, or even the young man just now—set them in motion, gave them life? Why does she see herself, always, as linked and attached? Yet so alone in reality.

Or maybe truly enchained? And of course deluding herself even about that. Refusing life by constantly taking its measure, rejecting life's joy with these damnable endless musings. And so many questions! Like now— as if failure or success, linked or alone are the only possible paths in life! Pondering endless abstractions here on a busy sidewalk, chockablock full of people, and so many miles from home.

But where *is* home? And what is a "self" after all? An entity as flat as a paper doll and as trapped? Part of one long chain? Blindly enchained forever unless you dropped hands and opened your eyes? That sweet and charming abstraction not really singers, but something else entirely? Something far darker?

Racists? Was that her chain? *Racists?*

Of course. Herself. The "song" for which her mouth widened into its narrow *O* not music, but only a captive's sorrowful and stylized moan? Her head full of unacknowledged fears about mixed-race grandchildren. Yes. Of course.

Herself: a racist. Her face burned with the shame of it, the truth: *a racist.*

And she was recalling what must have been her first sight of a black person. Or at least her first consciousness of what humans call "race." Maybe fifty years ago, in Tulsa.

She'd probably been four years old, so yes, more than fifty years ago. She and her mother were on a downtown bus, standing up. A crowded bus. So maybe heading back home from a rare trip downtown? A very crowded bus. And a boy about her size got on with a man, probably his father, so most likely the man was the same color, the same "race," though she doesn't recall any details about the man, the father.

The boy's size most likely was what inspired her: a lovely boy exactly her own size and height. An amazing boy suddenly entering her world, climbing onto the bus to stand near her, almost beside her. So she'd proudly shouted it out. At least that's what she remembers. But maybe she actually said it softly? She was as quiet and introspective a child as she is an adult. One who tried hard to please. So, probably, she only tugged hard at her mother's hand, tugged Mama's hand and spoke out loud, audibly, in awe: "Look, Mama! A chocolate boy!"

Surely she'd spoken in wonder: amazement, pure delight, she's certain.

Her mother had squeezed her hand hard; she recalls that too: probably hoping to silence her. "White people" were most likely the only people she knew then. Not that her family was overtly racist, and they certainly did *not* intend to be racist. But most likely their daily world, and hers, was common to people like themselves at the time: separate and unequal lives. Inadvertent. Unexamined. Why she's remained an inadvertent racist?

And the face of the boy: she remembers it clearly. Wounded, but brave. He'd frowned right into her eyes, stared deep into her eyes without looking away, frowning hard, staring back. Maybe she'll recall that look of his forever. Recalling it like this, so suddenly, she's certain she will. Such an amazing look of triumphant injury to appear on a child's face: his lips pursed, his eyes cold but proud, full of such cold dignity, his forehead crinkling hard with a slight and very dignified cold frown, staring back into her eyes. He understood something far larger than themselves, as she did not, an evil he rejected. She, of course, had *not* intended to say or do, or *be*, anything but an admiring fellow creature.

But a racist nonetheless. He'd known. Four years old. The message in his eyes.

The same evil her grandchildren-to-be would someday be forced to experience in this world? *Ah, but not if I have anything to say about it!*

No! No one had better dare treat any grandchild of hers unfairly!

Not even herself! Least of all herself. She'll learn from this day, she vows.

It *is* possible. She'll change: not a fatalist at all. And maybe that was the gift life was giving her? The chance to grow? Was that what Marl was granting her? An opportunity to change? To be fully alive again? Anyway, she will not go one step further in this life as a racist!

Rena moved forward on the sidewalk, turning so Celia couldn't see. And she felt a vast future spreading before her like a golden trail—she saw it all: Celie choosing a man she loves. Marl and Royce with children—two, no, maybe *three*—a wealth of grandchildren whose skin color is absolutely beside the point. Children she loves with all her heart.

And the shop. She was missing it again. *Life.* Her own life, moving forward as it must.

The dollar in her hand, its paper worn and soft, so well used, was a shock to her fingers. Another gift, bringing her back to Seattle: to *now*, knowing exactly what she must do. This reclaimed dollar would become her soul's kite. A promise. A small humble thing set free. Rena felt the crumpled bill stretch out in her fingers and rise. Cold air filled her lungs as the dollar fluttered, taking the wind—then it was up and caught, released: twirling, spinning, rising, and soaring away.

About the Author

Jean Anderson is the author of another collection of short stories, *In Extremis and Other Alaskan Stories* (Plover Press, 1989), and coeditor of the regional anthology *Inroads: Alaska's 27 Fellowship Writers* (Alaska State Council on the Arts, 1988). She and her husband came to Fairbanks in 1966. Anderson was a founding staff member and early editor of the journal *Permafrost* at the University of Alaska Fairbanks, where as a mature student she earned her BA and MFA then taught English for a decade. Anderson's fiction has appeared in anthologies and in *Alaska Quarterly Review, The Alaska Reader, Cirque, Chariton Review, Connotations, Kalliope, Northern Review, Permafrost, Prairie Schooner,* and elsewhere. She has also written poems, essays, two plays, and many book reviews and enjoys being part of Alaska's literary world.

Anderson's work has received a number of awards, including a PEN Syndicated Fiction selection, an Individual Artist Award in Literature from the Alaska State Council on the Arts, a Lila Wallace Foundation award, plus local and regional prizes and a month-long writer's residency in Sitka from The Island Institute. *Human Being Songs* was a finalist for BkMk Press's 2015 Sharat Chandra Prize for Short Fiction, judged by Marge Piercy, at the University of Missouri-Kansas City.